DAMN
YANKEES

By Douglass Wallop

Night Light
The Year the Yankees Lost the Pennant
The Sunken Garden
What Has Four Wheels and Flies
So This Is What Happened to Charlie Moe
On Popular Music in America
Ocean Front
The Mermaid in the Swimming Pool
Baseball: An Informal History
Stone
Howard's Bag
Mixed Singles
The Other Side of the River
Regatta

DAMN YANKEES

A NOVEL BY

DOUGLASS WALLOP

W · W · NORTON & COMPANY

NEW YORK · LONDON

ISBN 0-393-31266-6

W. W. Norton & Company, Inc.
500 Fifth Avenue, New York, N.Y. 10110
W. W. Norton & Company Ltd.
10 Coptic Street, London WC1A 1PU

PRINTED IN THE UNITED STATES OF AMERICA

1 2 3 4 5 6 7 8 9 0

DAMN
YANKEES

| 1 | On the hot and humid night of July 21, 1958, when all signs pointed to a tenth consecutive pennant for the New York Yankees, a manhole cover rose slowly from its resting place |

near the center of a certain intersection in Washington, D. C. A moment later the dark-clad figure of a man climbed gingerly up to the street. Dusting himself off and replacing the cover, he walked over to a street light, where he pulled a slip of paper from his pocket, studied it intently for a few seconds, and then hurried away.

It was on the same night that Joe Boyd, a middle-aged real estate salesman, met the man who was to change the course of his life and, indirectly, the standings of the American League. Joe had no forewarning; he was not even aware of the man's corporeal existence. The meeting was a complete surprise.

The Yankees, fresh from a triumphant series in Chicago, were in the city of Cleveland that night, while the Washington Senators were in Detroit, engaging the Tigers in a game of little meaning except to the most grimly devoted followers of the two teams; and these, as the years passed, were becoming fewer. The Tigers were currently the fifth-place team; the Senators were in sixth and moving toward seventh, their customary habitat, with all the singleness of purpose of a homing pigeon.

Joe Boyd, one of the grimly devoted followers, was sitting alone in the dark on his screened side porch, listening with despair and disgust to a radio broadcast of the game. It was now the top of the seventh and the Tigers were leading by seven runs.

When the Senators failed to score in the seventh, Joe muttered, "What's the matter with you guys anyway?" and, shaking his head, turned on a lamp and picked up the evening paper, already folded to the sports page.

With no pleasure, he reread an account of the Yankees' victory over the Chicago White Sox the previous day, a victory which gave the Yankees a sweep of the three-game series and moved them out ahead of the White Sox, the second-place club, by seven and a half games.

The article included a statement by Mr. Kevin Bromwell, the New York manager, to the following effect: "We've got our work cut out for us. Those Sox are a fired-up bunch of guys. We'll give it everything we got, but I have a sneaky feeling this may be the year."

When Joe read this he grunted in derision, just as he had grunted upon reading the same statement in the morning paper. What Mr. Bromwell meant, Joe knew, was that this might be the year the fantastic Yankee winning streak came a cropper. Or this, at any rate, was what Mr. Bromwell wanted people to think he meant. Joe knew he didn't mean it. He'd been saying things like that for years—in fact, ever since he had taken over the managerial reins from Mr. Casey Stengel.

Whether Bromwell talked this way out of superstition or

because of a charitable nature was debatable. It was perhaps more likely out of self-interest for, as Joe's favorite sports columnist was fond of noting, it would be self-defeating for the Yankees to show open contempt for the seven other teams which continued so steadfastly to accommodate them by showing up on opening day each year.

While the Tigers still batted, Joe also read over a letter to the sports editor containing another in a long series of fan suggestions on how to keep the Yankees from winning another pennant. This advocated that a Yankee player hitting a home run should be compelled to circle the bases five times at top speed and thereby exhaust himself. Yesterday somebody had suggested that the Yankees be forced to carry weights, like jockeys. It had become a game, this search, but it was a game that Joe found distasteful. To him, it was a form of cringing.

Tossing the paper aside, he turned off the lamp and gave his attention once more to the radio, for the Senators were coming up in the eighth. The first batter singled, and Joe's imagination quickly constructed a rally which would send his team in front. His reverie was snapped by the second batter, who grounded into a double play, and by Mrs. Boyd, who was calling from their bedroom:

"Isn't it over yet, Joe?"

"Okay," he said, concentrating.

"I said isn't it over yet?"

"Almost."

"Are they losing?"

Joe grunted.

"Joe, are they losing?"

"Yes, they're losing."

"That's strange," she said sarcastically, and when he didn't reply, she said, "Well, I'm going to turn off my light now. Are you coming up soon?"

Joe grunted.

Bess's attitude toward his feeling for baseball ranged from tolerance to sarcasm—tolerant during the early season and steadily less sympathetic as the summer wore on and the humidity mounted. Often, most recently the day before yesterday, she told him with scorn that he, a grown man, should be ashamed to let the fortunes of a baseball team, and a feckless one at that, mean so much in his life; and that he should be particularly ashamed to spend between two and three hours every night watching the telecast of home games and listening to the broadcast of those away.

"Why, if you added up the number of hours you've spent in your life watching and listening to baseball games, there's no end to the things you could have done with that time," she was fond of saying. "You could have built a bridge or read all the greatest books."

"This is my relaxation," was Joe's usual answer. At other times, when his humor was not good, he would reply with some heat, "So what if I never build a bridge or read all the greatest books? Who says I have to?"

"If you had *been* a baseball player it might be different," she sometimes said.

If he had been a baseball player . . . He often thought of the time when he was a sophomore in high school. He had planned to go out for the team. But on the day practice started, a girl—whose name he had since forgotten but to whom he was deeply attached at the time—asked him to walk home from school with her. He didn't go out for the team that day . . . nor the next . . . nor ever. It was on such small hinges of fate that a man's whole career swung. But for that girl, he might have been a major-league star. He had a deft pair of hands, a good sense of co-ordination . . . It was true that he had never been much at hitting a curve, but that was a deficiency that could have been overcome with practice . . .

The team did not score in the eighth inning, and this time while the Tigers were batting he let the light remain off and sprawled back in the old rocker, thinking that it had been a tough day all around. The weather had been miserable, still was, but that wasn't all. Ever since returning from his vacation he had been working hard on a house which the owner had listed at $28,000. This morning he had gotten a signed contract for an offer of $27,500. First he had phoned but there was no answer. Then, counting his commission and unmindful of the heat, Joe had driven five miles in a spirit of conquest and waited on the front porch; but when the owner arrived he said no, he wouldn't take $27,500, and furthermore, after giving it some thought, he had decided to take the house off the market.

That was life, and life this summer had not been good. There were a number of reasons he might blame; the one he blamed most often, and blamed again now as the lead-off Tiger doubled down the left-field line, was that he had taken his vacation too early. With unreasoning impatience, he had selected the two weeks and three days ending July 5; he should have had better sense, for he had returned to heat and humidity that would not end until near October.

It was a lousy vacation. He had been trying not to admit this, but in a flash of irritation he suddenly admitted it now.

Certainly it had not been a vacation to treasure in the memory; this he knew. But there was something very painful about admitting that your one vacation of the year had been downright lousy. Yet, this he was now admitting, in a small explosion of anger, ignited partly by Bess's sarcasm and partly, he knew, by the Detroit player's double. Setting the old rocker in motion, he tried to convince himself that it was not so; that, as he had told the crew at the office, it was a "pretty darn nice trip, all things considered." But conviction came hard.

It was a repeat vacation, the same motor trip to Quebec that he and Bess had first taken in 1956 and had taken both years since, going up by way of Vermont and New Hampshire, returning along the coast through Maine and Massachusetts. The scenery had not changed. All the familiar landmarks were in place. Yet something was lacking. Perhaps it was the absence of Ruth, their daughter, who had been married in February and was now living with her husband on an army base in Oklahoma. Perhaps it was simply that three years of the same vacation were too many.

Whatever the cause, the trip had been neither relaxing nor inspiring, and he realized that it was foolish to pretend otherwise. On the way up they had paused as usual for a look at the Great Stone Face but he had barely glanced at it, had waited impatiently in the car while Bess foraged about the crowded souvenir shack for trinkets bearing the Great Stone Face motif. For the third consecutive year he said yes when she asked if they could stop and go through a certain well-advertised cavern, but quickly and emphatically changed his mind when they arrived to find that an extra charge was being made this season for the compulsory attire of sneakers and coveralls. Looking across the river at Quebec as the ferry pulled out from the slip, he had not found the vista so picturesque as he remembered it; nor, on the return trip, had he enjoyed searching out places approved by Duncan Hines. One evening, as eight o'clock approached, he had become so impatient as to insist they eat in a roadside seafood shack. He found his patience thinner than usual when Bess tarried long over the selection of post cards, or when she gave the fluttering cries signaling that she had spied a sign telling of the imminence of an antique shop. The most depressing aspect of all, however, had little to do with either Bess or the route: This was buying the daily paper of a different city each day and watching, helpless, while the Senators skidded from fourth to fifth and then to sixth place.

The Tigers scored one in the eighth. In the ninth, now eight runs behind, Joe's team went out one, two, three. As soon as the last batter was retired, he switched off the radio, not even waiting to hear the totals. Tonight he didn't want to hear the totals.

Slumping again, he began to rock gently. A breeze rustled through the maple next door and moved on to soothe his face. He sighed, expectant, wishing the breeze in motion again, but it died; now there was no sound in the suburban neighborhood except, very faintly . . . He listened and was sure he heard the sound of a hose a couple of doors away. That would be the Everetts' house. Old man Everett was stealthily watering his lawn, or at the very least was sprinkling his azaleas, hoping no one would hear and report him, for there had been such a dry spell that watering lawns and shrubs and washing cars was prohibited until the next good rain. Joe's own lawn that he had nurtured so carefully was baked to a brown stubble and would surely have to be reseeded in the fall. If the fall ever came . . .

The breeze returned and he leaned back gratefully, offering his face. When it disappeared, he rose stiffly, stretched, and set out from the house for the short walk he took every evening just before bed.

Old man Everett was sitting on his front stoop, hose in hand, the house dark behind him. Joe paused. "I think I'll report you tomorrow," he said.

"All right, you old so and so," Mr. Everett said, "you report me and I'll report Bess's bridge club for making such a racket last night."

Joe chuckled and Old Man Everett chuckled, and Joe called, "Do you think it'll ever rain?"

"Forecast is for fair and hot."

Joe grunted and walked on. It was now after eleven o'clock. Most of the houses were dark. Familiar houses. He knew what each looked like at every season of the year.

Across the street, from the opposite direction, came old Mr. Thatcher, walking his dog, and, as always, talking to it. "All right, old man, it's all right," Joe could hear him say. And then: "Would you like that? Would you?"

Joe walked on, thinking of how many years he had heard Old Man Thatcher saying that to his dog; this dog and others.

He had turned two corners of the block and was nearing the bottom of the long hill when, with a quickening of his heart, he saw the dark-clad figure of a man step suddenly from the shadows.

2 Joe stopped short, but after a second of silent self-encouragement forced his legs forward again, wondering if he was about to be robbed and then remembering with relief that he had left his wallet on the bureau.

"Good evening, Mr. Boyd," the man said.

"Good evening," Joe said, mystified that his name was known. He hurried on, but the man fell into step beside him, and as they neared a street lamp, Joe took a sidelong glance. Although even at this hour the temperature was still over ninety and the humidity unworldly, the stranger wore a black topcoat, the lapels turned up and crossed to hide his chin and mouth. A black hat was pulled low over his brow.

"How did the team make out tonight?" the stranger asked.

They had reached the corner now and Joe halted. "You mean the baseball team?" he said.

"Naturally."

"They lost. Eleven to three."

The stranger made a clucking noise of sympathy. "That's a shame," he said. "It must be hard for you."

Joe found the man's voice singular. Although its owner seemed trying very hard for an effect of mellifluous cordiality he was gravely handicapped for it was a deeply rasping voice, at times hoarse.

"I'm used to it by now," Joe said. He paused, scraping his shoe against the curb. "Or partly used to it, anyway."

"And incidentally, how was your trip to Quebec this year?" the stranger asked, disregarding Joe's question.

"It wasn't bad," Joe said. "Say, do you live around here? I don't remember seeing you before. Where do you get all your information, anyway?" He looked up the street to see if Old Man Thatcher and his dog were returning, but they were not in sight.

"I was reading through your file," the stranger said.

"My file!"

"Sure. Your file. We have a file on quite a few of you older fellows."

"Who is we, if you don't mind my asking?"

The stranger chuckled. "My name is Applegate, but that's of no importance," he said. "What's important right at the moment is that punk baseball team you've been rooting for all these years."

"I wouldn't call them punk exactly," Joe said, and a coolness came into his voice.

"And conversely, it is the New York Yankees who are also important," the stranger said. "You say you wouldn't call that team of yours punk? Let me ask you how long it's been since they won the pennant."

"Well, let's see . . ."

"It's fast approaching three decades," the stranger said. "Am I right? Now if the file is accurate, and—"

"I don't get this file stuff," Joe broke in.

". . . and there's no reason to believe it's anything less, you were just short of twenty-five at the time they last won, and now you're fifty. Did it ever occur to you that you may even die before you see them win the pennant again? For that matter you may die before any team other than the Yankees wins it. There's something rather tragic about that, something very sad."

Joe admitted that it was so, although he did not reply.

"On your death bed," the stranger went on, "it would be very sad to think back and realize—well, I mean this period of barrenness spans the best years of your life . . . all those years in the second division, you know what I mean."

"They just picked up a couple of pretty good pitchers on waivers," Joe said. "I think they'll probably pull themselves together in a few days."

The stranger chuckled scornfully. "Just like every spring you read they're bringing up some hot rookies from the minors and this year it's going to be different, eh, Mr. Boyd? Only it never is."

"Maybe so and maybe not," Joe said, "but you still haven't explained what you mean by my file. What kind of a file? I'm no communist."

"Communist?" The stranger began laughing without control, finally saying weakly, "Communist! What memories that stirs! No, of course you're not a communist."

"Well, then what are you talking about?"

For a few seconds longer the stranger laughed. Then,

straightening to his full height, he folded the lapels of his coat more carefully over his chin and touched his nose lightly. "Mr. Boyd," he said, "I've got a proposition for you. How would you like to be a baseball player?"

"A baseball player? Where? In the old men's softball league?"

"In the American League, Mr. Boyd. Playing for that team of yours. You can be Moses and lead them out of the wilderness, to use a metaphor I've never particularly cared for."

"Was it a good party?" Joe asked.

"What do you mean, was it a good party?"

"That party you went on tonight. It must have been good."

"Don't make light, Mr. Boyd," the stranger said sternly. "My time isn't so plentiful that I can spend it in levity."

"You mean when you say I can be a baseball player I should take you seriously?" Joe asked.

"Very seriously."

"How's all this going to happen?"

"It's easy," the stranger said. "Just say the word and you can be the finest baseball player in the world."

"But how? I'm fifty years old. Besides I was never much good at baseball anyway. This is ridiculous."

"Age is a very flexible thing," the stranger said. "You don't have to be fifty years old, you know. What's most important is the will to be a good baseball player. And Mr. Boyd, in all this country we've never found anybody with as great a will as yours."

"Listen, who are you, for heaven's sake?" Joe demanded.

"Not exactly," the stranger said. "But as I told you before, my name is Applegate."

"Well, Mr. Applegate," Joe said, starting off, "I suggest you see a doctor. Or at least go sleep it off."

Joe heard the low chuckle following him up the block. Then it seemed to overtake him and a moment later his heart pounded violently. Just ahead, a dark figure stepped from the shadows.

"Now as I was saying, Mr. Boyd," the stranger began, and then chuckled again. "I'm sorry I startled you, my friend," he went on. "But there's certainly no reason to be startled. I have nothing but friendly intentions. My only wish is to help you lead a more fruitful life. Now if you'll just stand still a second or two so I can make myself clear. . . . Cigarette?"

Joe declined and a second later felt his body again grow weak. The stranger had lit his own cigarette but not by match or lighter. He had merely snapped his fingers.

"Now then," he said, "suppose we find a place to sit down and talk this over. Here's a bench up at the corner. Let's have a seat."

Joe looked and there was a bench next to the bus-stop sign, although to his certain knowledge there had never been a bench there before.

"By the way," the stranger said, settling himself and stretching his legs, "do you mind if I call you Joe? And you can call me App, if you like. That's what my friends call me. . . . Come on, Joe, have a seat."

Joe stood a moment longer and then gingerly sat down, as far away from Applegate as the width of the bench permitted. A few blocks away he could see the lights of a bus approaching, and it was a welcome sight. His strength was returning. His jaw tightened. He would now restore the whole interview to normalcy. With a calm phrase or two . . . He could, instead, get up and go home, but that seemed cowardly on the face of it. There was no reason to go home. It was nothing but normal. The man was drunk. The fire had started—well, he could have been lighting a kitchen match with his thumbnail. And he had simply run along through the shrubbery. That's how he had gotten ahead again so quickly.

On the strength of these self-assurances, Joe squared his shoulders and asked, "What kind of liquor were they feeding you tonight?" But his voice quavered and lacked conviction. The bus sped past without stopping.

"Oh, come now, Joe," Applegate said. "Let's not be sophomoric about this. Let's get down to business. Now first of all I'd like to ask you a question. How long has it been since you ran?"

"Ran?"

"Sure, ran."

"I don't know. I can't remember exactly."

"Will you do me a favor, Joe? Stand up, if you will. Now walk a few steps away. That's right. Now head back down the block the way we came from. Good! Now—run!"

"I don't feel like running," Joe said.

"Well, just jog a little. Just get yourself started."

Joe began to jog, and then, suddenly, as though beyond his own will, he was running at great speed. His body felt light; indeed it felt thin. Thin and hard and wiry. In mid-flight he thumped his stomach. It was flat as a board, and as hard. It was not his own stomach, he thought headily, but all the better. Breathing easily, his head reared back, he tasted something from the distant past: The way the air had felt, warm spring air as he remembered it, rushing past his head; the sense of headlong flight, a feeling he had not experienced since—since the last time he had run, and that was not since his youth.

At the end of the block he stopped, and when he touched his stomach it was again his own. Flabby.

"Now run back," Applegate called.

Joe began running, but slowly, sluggishly, with heavy legs. After only a few steps he was breathing hard. His temples pounded. His stomach quivered out ahead of him. He clenched his fists and dug harder, but he could not recapture the swiftness of the trip down and already he missed it.

"Out of condition, Joe?" Applegate asked sympathetically, as Joe finally arrived. "How did it feel on the way down, though?"

Gasping, Joe sank to the bench, fearful of the strain on his heart. He shouldn't have done it. And yet, going down, it had seemed no strain at all. "It felt good," he managed to say.

"You could run like that all the time," Applegate said. "The question is, would you like it?"

"You mean be able to run like that?" Joe asked, still panting.

"Yes, and more besides. To have your youth, to have almost unheard of skill in baseball—to be able to carry that team of yours on your back—all the way to the pennant."

Joe stood, trying to suck in deep breaths, looking off toward the corner store—in his earliest memory a meat market, later a dry goods and notions store, once a cleaning and pressing place, and now, about to become something else. He saw a man and woman moving about, placing things on shelves.

"You mean you're trying to tell me they could still win the pennant this season?" he asked.

"Sure, it's not too late. A couple of good winning streaks for you boys and a little tough luck for the Yankees—that's all it would take."

"That's ridiculous," Joe said between pantings.

"It's not ridiculous, boy. It can be done. Just trust in me."

"And who are you?" Joe asked again, although by now he thought perhaps he knew.

"Applegate is the name. A-P-P—" he broke off and chuckled. "I told you that was of no importance, my boy. The question is—do you accept?"

Another bus was approaching. This one stopped and a woman got off.

"Oh, good evening, Mr. Boyd," she said.

"Good evening, Mrs. Stewart."

"What are you doing standing here on the corner all by yourself?" she asked.

It was not until then that Joe saw Applegate was gone.

"Oh, just getting a little air," he said.

The woman started off. "Do you think it will ever rain?" she called back. Joe didn't answer and her heels clicked off up the hill, out of hearing.

"Hey," Joe called. Then, "Where are you, Applegate? Hey, *Applegate*."

There was no answer, no sign. Joe looked about in each direction, peering into the shadows, and when he turned back, the bench too had disappeared.

3 Joe dropped to the edge of his twin bed (Bess was snoring complacently in hers) and began pulling off his socks, then paused; still grasping the heel of one, he stared abstractedly into a shaft of moonlight that reached across the floor and climbed the radiator to touch Bess's sewing basket.

Of course it had happened. Beyond the shadow of a doubt it had happened. Not only that, but he knew who Applegate was and what he was offering and the usual strings attached. And the time had already come, Joe told himself, to stop being coy, to cut out all this awe-struck baloney about whether it had or hadn't happened and decide what he was going to do about it.

That is, if he got a chance to do anything at all about it. Thirty minutes had passed since Applegate's disappearance, and maybe he wouldn't be back.

Joe continued to undress. The fantastic thing wasn't that Applegate should have asked *some*body; the fantastic thing was that it should have been Joe Boyd. Why Joe Boyd? Unless, as Applegate had said, or clearly intimated, it was his love of baseball. That was all. It was comforting, at any rate, to know that it wasn't because he had established a reputation for evil.

And yet, the evil aspect of it seemed the least consideration of all, he thought, pulling on his pajama pants. Could an aim so worthy as denying the Yankees a tenth consecutive pennant be evil?

Furthermore, it was flattering in a sense to have been chosen, and considered from the same angle perhaps it was his duty to respond: His duty to all the long-suffering legions who, like himself, yearned for the Yankees' downfall; and to the scanter legions who yearned for the renascence of the Senators. Given the same opportunity, he told himself, most would have embraced it on the spot, without the shillyshallying he had displayed back there a few minutes ago at the bus stop.

It was a worthy cause. That much was established. And he must admit that his feelings were not entirely altruistic. There would be glory in it for himself.

He walked into the bathroom. It was like a crusade. And a crusade, by its very nature, meant glory as well as sacrifice.

With pajama jacket off, he stood before the bathroom mirror, appraising his body closely for the first time in years, sharply aware of its spent tissue, its gray, grizzled appearance, and of the thin, moist film over his chest and shoulders, relic of the day's humidity.

So far as he and Bess were concerned, it was true that they had come to the end of something. Not of marriage, necessarily, but of an era. Ever since Ruth had left home, things had been different. There seemed less purpose. He and Bess were more conscious of themselves and of each other. A little sabbatical wouldn't hurt. He had often heard it said that when a husband and wife have a little vacation from each other they're much better for it.

Sabbatical! He grunted.

Thirty years they had been married, and that made it much more than a sabbatical. A quadruple sabbatical, at the very least.

A baseball player . . . He stared into the mirror's reflection of his rather meek eyes and tried to bring into them a glint of determination.

But, a voice warned, it could mean jeopardizing your whole future.

Well, he concluded, getting into bed, in the final analysis it would depend on what kind of deal he could make with this Applegate. He mustn't appear too eager. And, as he always told himself when approaching a real-estate deal, you are not to be disappointed no matter which way it turns out. Either way would have its compensations.

That *if:* if he ever saw Applegate again.

For a long while he lay on one elbow. Bess snored on. A breeze, in motion at last, stirred the curtains. He heard the clock strike one.

When finally he closed his eyes he felt the turf beneath spiked shoes; it was like sponge, resilient, giving his feet wings. And he must have dozed, because he saw a monster with a bloated, insatiable face, across its swollen chest the word YANKEES. He was striking the face with a baseball bat.

Just before the clock struck two, he was wakened by a sharp, unmistakable pang of hunger. He slipped from bed to pad barefoot downstairs and through the silent rooms to the kitchen.

"Hiya, Joe."

He had opened the door of the refrigerator and grasped a quart of milk when the voice rasped behind him. He jumped, turned, and there, dimly outlined in the light from beneath the ice-cube compartment, was Applegate, seated patiently at the kitchen table.

"I'm sorry, Joe. I always seem to be scaring you. Now where were we?"

Unsteadily, Joe put the milk bottle on the table. "How did you get in?" he asked. "The doors were locked."

"Oh well," Applegate said airily. "You know how it is . . . Say, how about pouring me a little of that milk, will you, Joe? Thanks. Incidentally, I'm sorry I had to run out on you but I had an emergency call."

Unsettled in spite of himself, Joe sat gingerly at the table across from Applegate and for a few seconds both sipped their milk in silence. With the refrigerator door closed, the kitchen now was in darkness, except for a faint glow from the alley, silhouetting Bess's favorite crape myrtle against the window.

Finishing his milk, Applegate expelled his breath in a sigh of deep satisfaction and said, "So as I believe I was saying, how about it?"

"You mean about the baseball?" Joe said.

"Of course."

"Well, I don't know. I won't say I'm disinterested exactly, but on the other hand . . ."

"You sound like one of your own prospects," Applegate said.

"No, that's got nothing to do with it," Joe said. "It's just —well, there are so many angles to be considered."

"Like what?"

"Well, for instance, what would happen to me, Joe Boyd?"

"Why, you'd be with the team, of course."

"I mean this me. So far as my wife and my job are concerned, I'd just disappear? Is that it?"

"Well, yes," Applegate said.

"Forever?"

"Well, that's one way of putting it, yes."

"And what happens after I stop being a baseball player? Then where would I be?"

"Well, now, of course, that's fairly well known," Applegate said. "Let's not belabor it, shall we?"

"You mean I'd be in it forever?"

"You might express it that way, yes."

"Then it's out of the question," Joe said with finality.

"But listen, Joe—"

"Do you mind keeping your voice down a little?" Joe said. "I don't want Mrs. Boyd to wake up."

"Sure. I'm sorry. This voice of mine is a problem sometimes." Applegate sighed. "Say, you haven't got a snack of something or other in that ice box, have you? I haven't had anything to eat since lunch, and when I don't have anything on my stomach I'm a little testy."

Joe peered into the refrigerator. "It looks pretty bare

in here," he said. "Wait a minute, here's some tomato aspic. Would you like that?"

"No, I never cared much for tomato aspic," Applegate said. "You wouldn't have any cheese, would you?"

"Nope." Joe rummaged, and a bent lid fell from a jelly jar to a lower shelf. "Wait, here's some molded tuna fish left over from Mrs. Boyd's bridge club last night."

"Okay, I guess I'll have that," Applegate said without enthusiasm. "Thanks. Well, whatever—oh, thanks," he said as Joe gave him a spoon. "Well, as I was about to say, I don't know what your decision's going to be, but there's one thing I can say for you, Joe. You're not taking a holier-than-thou attitude about all this. Some of the guys you run into . . . They really rub me the wrong way."

For a while he ate in silence and then said, "So you're not willing to consider it on a permanent basis, right?"

"That much is definite," Joe said.

"Well . . ." Applegate toyed with his spoon and then chuckled in exasperation. "Sometimes I really don't understand you guys," he said. "Take you, for instance. Here you've never been anywhere in your life except Quebec and the Luray Caverns . . ."

"That's not entirely true," Joe said. "We've been to Atlantic City and Williamsburg and . . ."

"Okay, so you've been to Atlantic City and Williamsburg." Sighing again, Applegate got to his feet. "Well, if that's your attitude, I guess I'm wasting my time. That's your final decision, right?"

"That's the way it has to be," Joe said, and for a second he thought Applegate was leaving, but he stood at the back door, peering out into the yard.

"That's a nice crape myrtle," he said absently; and then, turning back to Joe, said: "It's not as though you'd be doing something so remarkable, you know. There's nothing so unique about it. I mean, how do you suppose some of those guys in the Senate got their start? And parking-lot owners?" He sat down again. "Just tell me your reasoning on it. That's what I'd like to know."

"Well, just on general principles I've always been against anything drawn up in perpetuity," Joe said. "That's one thing. Then there's my wife. I've got her to consider."

"Your wife?" Applegate snorted. "You've been considering her for thirty years, and the closest you ever got to any kind of he-man adventure was cutting your finger opening a bottle of salad dressing."

"Nevertheless . . ." Joe said.

Applegate drummed his fingers impatiently on the table. "Joe, Joe," he said and sighed. "The trouble is, you're a nice guy. I'd have been out of here twenty minutes ago if you hadn't been such a nice guy."

"Now if you should give me something with an escape clause, I might consider it," Joe said.

"Escape clause," Applegate muttered. "Escape clause, my foot!"

"Okay."

"Hey, where you going?"

"I'm going to bed," Joe said, turning back to put the milk glasses and the tin mold in the sink.

"Wait a minute now—don't rush off," Applegate said. "Don't go getting precipitate on me."

"If we're not going to have a meeting of minds I might as well get some sleep."

"Wait a minute now," Applegate repeated. He started to speak, checked himself and turned again to the door.

"It was an interesting talk, anyway," Joe said.

Applegate turned with a rueful chuckle. "Boy, I'd hate to be a real-estate man trying to sell you something. Okay, come on, sit down. I guess half a loaf is better than none. What's your deal?"

"Something on a temporary basis," Joe said. "The principal thing is this. If I don't like it, I'm entitled to call the whole thing off."

"That's highly irregular," Applegate said, "but as I said before about the half a loaf . . ."

"Well, on that basis I think I might be willing to have a whack at it," Joe said.

Applegate leaped to his feet. "Good boy, Joe! Splendid." His voice was not the voice of one who had just been bested in a bargain, and Joe suddenly felt deep misgivings. "Here's what I propose we do," Applegate went on. "Suppose we get the ball rolling right away."

"Remember," Joe said. "Temporary."

"Sure, temporary. I said temporary, didn't I? So, like I say, let's get rolling right away. Let's not take the time to go into the fine print tonight. Suppose we just enter into a gentleman's agreement tonight, all on a tentative basis, and then in a few days we can iron out the details. Okay? Because I think it's important that you get to the team as soon as possible. Now then, just give me your hand and we'll shake on it. No, the other hand."

Applegate's palm was moist and his handshake of the limp-fish variety, but Joe was not to think of these things until later. The victory in terms was one he was now not sure he wanted. He felt a sudden fear and, dropping Applegate's hand, stepped back, expecting catastrophe.

But nothing happened.

"You mean that's all there is to it?" he said.

"Sure," Applegate said. "What did you expect to do—sign your name in blood, or some phony stunt like that? This is the twentieth century, man."

"Okay, if you say so."

Applegate laughed. "Don't be so solemn about it, Joe. Come on now, we've got work to do."

"You haven't got a deal where I could be both places at once, have you?" Joe asked.

"Unfortunately, no," Applegate said. "If we had one, we'd *really* be flourishing. Come on now, Joe, let's move."

"I'll have to write my wife a note," Joe said.

"All right. Tell her you heard gold has been discovered in Kentucky." Applegate laughed. "That's really not so funny, though, come to think of it. Okay now. Get ready. I'm going out after a cab and make your plane reservation. I'll be back in ten minutes."

With pounding heart, Joe climbed the stairs silently. Bess snored on. He felt his throat lump up as he stood above the bed, looking down at her rumpled gray hair, barely visible in the faint light. "So long, old girl." He formed the words silently.

In the bathroom he began the note:

"Dear old girl," he wrote, and then paused. Dear old girl, indeed! Last night she had threatened to throw the radio in the alley if he listened to the game while the bridge girls were there. He tore up the sheet and began another:

"Dear Bess: When you wake up, I will be gone. I can't tell you where, so please trust me. Don't get the police. Don't be nervous. It won't be for too long, and when I come back we'll be rich, probably. Please call the office and tell them I'm taking a leave of absence to go see my sick brother in Minnesota unexpectedly. I will send all the money you need. Don't forget the real-estate taxes are due on the house next week. Please pay them. This has nothing to do with any other woman. You know I wouldn't want anybody but my old girl, in spite of everything. Love, Joe."

He felt tears begin as he wrote the last sentence. For long moments, he sat there on the edge of the bathtub, staring at the sheet of paper, finally scratching out the words, "in spite of everything." Perhaps it had not been easy for her, either.

Then he carried the note into their room and put it on the bureau, weighting it with one of her shoes.

The taxi was waiting a few houses down. Walking toward it, he was struck again by fear and halted in his tracks, looking back at the dark house.

"Come on, Joe," Applegate whispered hoarsely. "The meter's running up."

With a final look, Joe turned and walked slowly to the cab.

"I have your reservation on the four-forty-five plane," Applegate said as he got in. "You'll be in Detroit in time for breakfast and then—look out, Tigers!"

"You made good time," Joe said.

"Sure," Applegate said. "I have friends."

4

"Briggs Stadium," Joe said as he got into the taxi and then, waving briefly to Applegate, sat back expectantly.

They had shopped until one o'clock and lunched at the hotel. It was now about three.

"Just get in the cab and relax," had been Applegate's final instruction. "By the time you get to the ball park you'll be the new guy."

The new guy, they agreed, should have a different name, and their choice had been Joe Hardy because, as Applegate pointed out, it sounded rather athletic.

But it was still Joe Boyd who sat in the taxi. This was evident from the mirror which Joe, sitting on the edge of the seat, watched intently: Still Joe Boyd's gray hair and mild blue eyes, although not Joe Boyd's clothes. In the mirror, beneath the creased and grizzled chin and slack folds of throat showed now the collar of a white oxford button-down shirt and the knot of a black and yellow tie of regimental stripes, neither of which items Joe Boyd had ever worn but about which Applegate was insistent. Joe looked again at the rest of the outfit Applegate had assembled so finically—the gray flannel slacks and the shetland jacket, a soft tan in shade. The slacks were tight in the waist and seat, and the jacket too large in the shoulders, but Applegate said these matters would be taken care of as soon as he became the new guy.

The blocks were passing rapidly and Joe, his eye on the mirror again, asked, "How much farther now?"

"Just a few blocks more," the driver said.

Joe's brow furrowed. He lit a cigarette, dragged on it twice and flipped it out the window. "Okay, Applegate, okay, how about it?" he muttered, thinking again that a taxi was a ridiculous place to pick for the transformation, if indeed there was to be a transformation. At the same time he was struck by the thought that it was brash of him to talk to Applegate so disrespectfully. Yet, already, he seemed to have lost his awe of Applegate. To have spent the past few hours with him, to have watched his picayune attention to detail, to have listened to his endlessly detailed instructions, was to lose awe. For long minutes at a time he had caught himself thinking that this companion in shopping and later in luncheon was indeed nothing more than a man named Applegate.

The cab was cutting over to the curb lane and pulling to a stop.

The mirror still showed the face of Joe Boyd, and it was with irritation that Joe reached into his pocket for a bill. Still watching the mirror, he handed it to the driver over the seat.

It must have happened when he switched his glance to count the change the driver was dropping into his palm, for with the dropping of the last dime he saw a concerned expression pass over the driver's face. The quarter Joe returned as a tip was unnoticed.

He looked quickly at the mirror and then, grinning, got out and slammed the door. "Good luck, driver," he said in a vibrating voice and then headed for the ball-park entrance, carrying in his mind's eye the image of a young face, of close-cropped hair, blond as his had been blond in youth, of a face grown ruddy and flesh become firm and of eyes clear and snapping.

There had been a time, some years before, when he had taken his vacation with a guy in the office; his two weeks had fallen squarely athwart an antique show for which Bess had been committed months in advance to act as hostess-guide. Setting off on a poker and fishing trip, he had felt guilt and elation, and it was this combination, only with much more of each, that he felt now as he asked the way to the visiting team's dressing room and was directed along a concrete runway beneath the grandstand.

The teams were meeting in a twi-night doubleheader, starting at six o'clock.

Joe tried the door. It was locked and, dropping his equipment bag, he waited. Ten minutes passed. Assuring himself that no one was in sight, he jogged a distance down the runway, then broke into a sprint. Grinning, he returned to the doorway and did a few deep knee bends.

At four o'clock some of the players began to arrive, and in another few minutes Joe spied Mr. Benny van Buren, the Washington team's manager, hurrying along the runway, wearing a harassed look and, perhaps because of it, instantly recognizable from his pictures. Mr. van Buren was a man of a weathered, rather florid countenance, with sandy, tufted eyebrows. He had reached the door and his hand was on the knob before Joe spoke his name.

"I beg your pardon, Mr. van Buren, my name is Joe Hardy," Joe said, holding out his hand which, after a second's hesitation, Mr. van Buren shook without enthusiasm.

"What can I do for you, son?" he said.

"I'd like a tryout," Joe said, indicating the equipment bag at Mr. van Buren's feet. "I've got all my stuff right here."

Mr. van Buren looked from valise to Joe with eyes crinkled at the corners from many long nights of squinting at pop flies against light towers. They were the eyes of a man who has known great suffering, and Joe felt a wave of sympathy. In his playing days, Mr. van Buren had been a hell-for-leather third baseman, the best the team had ever had. Managing a seventh-place team these five years must have been gall.

"If I could just hit a couple while the team's taking batting practice," Joe went on as Mr. van Buren still hesitated. "That's all the time I'd need. Okay?"

"Where've you been playing, fella?" Mr. van Buren asked.

"Oh, here and there," Joe said, quickly adding, "I wouldn't take up more than a minute or two."

"Where is here and there?" Mr. van Buren persisted.

"Well, to be honest, it was mostly sandlot ball, but I can hit a ball quite a distance, I think."

"You think?"

"Well, I'm pretty sure."

At this point a swarthy individual with a dour expression approached.

"Hiya, Rocky, how's the wing?" Mr. van Buren asked.

The newcomer shook his head ruefully. "Wing's okay, Ben," he said, "but I've got a terrific headache. I don't think I'd better pitch tonight."

Mr. van Buren frowned. "Headache from what?" he asked.

"Well, it was so hot and I didn't feel like going out, so I was sitting up in the hotel room, watching TV most of the day, and it gave me a buster of a headache."

Again Mr. van Buren frowned, and Joe felt his own brow crease in sympathy with the manager. This must be Rocky Pratt, the guy everybody said had so much potential but who never delivered. With an attitude like this it was small wonder.

"I've tried aspirin," the indisposed pitcher went on, "but it didn't help."

Mr. van Buren looked up with an expression blended of disdain and hopelessness. "Okay," he said curtly, "suppose you pitch batting practice. Maybe it'll help your head." He turned to Joe. "Okay, kid, there's your man. Go out and let's see what you can do."

The pitcher shrugged and entered the dressing room. As Joe bent to pick up the bag, he was clapped on the shoulder, and Mr. van Buren was smiling. "That," he said, "in case you don't know it, son, was Mr. Rocky Pratt, and there's something very tragic about the case of Mr. Pratt. For five years he's been wanting us to trade him to the Yankees. Only—" and Mr. van Buren chuckled—"the Yankees don't want him."

Joe dressed uneasily, his back to the room, his face to the recesses of an empty locker, worried for a while that Applegate, with his already apparent fondness for bum jokes, might pull a switch on him, and he would be exposed before this group of stalwarts as a fifty-year-old real-estate salesman.

As a safeguard, he put on the baseball cap Applegate had provided, pulling its long peak low over his eyes and then listening, with growing surprise and some disappointment, to the conversation going on about the room. Without ever really thinking about it, he had always assumed that the men of a seventh-place team would be cast down in gloom. He had pictured them with clenched fists and teeth and narrowed eyes, somewhat the way he felt he himself looked as he listened to a baseball broadcast.

But around him there were only relatively happy sounds. A couple of guys were discussing TV programs they had known and two others their children. Somebody told a joke. Rocky Pratt was being addressed in a low voice by someone who laughed every few seconds. "Nuts," Pratt interpolated. Then the low voice and the laugh, and from Pratt: "Yeah? Oh, yeah? Nuts."

And now and then the sound of spiked shoes on concrete as one after another of the players finished dressing and headed for the field.

Joe shook his head, puzzled. The thrill would be less in bailing out a team bland in defeat. And then he remembered Mr. van Buren and felt better. Mr. van Buren was a man who cared.

Hanging on the inside of the locker door was a small mirror and, bending down, Joe took a look at the lean face beneath the peak of the cap. He liked what he saw, then thought again of Bess as she must have appeared when she read his note; he looked longer and still liked what he saw. It's only for a little while, he told himself, and I can go back if I like. That's the good part of it.

It was a glaringly hot afternoon, or should have been, Joe thought, as he walked out onto the field; and then he halted in his tracks, a smile spreading slowly over his face. It should have been apparent immediately, but not until now had he grasped it. Since the second he stepped from the taxi, he had felt neither heat nor humidity. Applegate was a man of many facets.

Still smiling, he looked around the park. Except for a few refreshment butchers, the stands were empty. A couple of guys were in the outfield shagging flies and a few others were fooling around the infield. The rest were still in the dressing room. Rocky Pratt was already on the hill, loosening up and pausing now and then to press the heel of his hand to his temple and shake his head vigorously.

Joe walked over to the dugout, picked up a bat and immediately put it down again, remembering all he had read about ball players and their favorite bats. A player was sitting in a corner of the dugout, clipping his nails. "Take one of those on the end," he said, not looking up.

"Thanks," Joe said, selected one, and headed for the plate.

The batting cage had been wheeled up and Pratt was firing them in hard. Joe watched, suddenly uneasy. Applegate now was far away, and although this might be a young man's body it was still Joe Boyd inside. Joe Boyd inside was at the moment very queasy. And there was still Joe Boyd's memory—the memory, for instance, of how Joe Boyd in his youth had been a terrible sucker for a roundhouse curve.

The ball came toward the plate like a bullet and hit the catcher's mitt with the report of a cannon.

Affecting nonchalance, Joe gazed toward the outfield, noticing on the scoreboard that the Yankees were leading the Indians six to one in the fifth.

That helped. Gripping the bat, he took a couple of practice swings and was surprised at the co-ordination in his muscles and at the way his stomach stretched tight as he pivoted.

"Okay," Pratt said.

Many hours before, Joe had decided that he would swing left-handed, and it was as a left-handed batter that he stepped now to the plate.

Pratt's first pitch zipped in under his wrists, and he stood with rooted spikes, not offering. Again the ball came in and once more he stood frozen. The catcher made a sound of impatience.

"There's nothing to it," Applegate had said. "All you gotta do is swing. I'll take care of the rest."

On the next pitch he swung. The ball soared on a line into deepest center field.

"Nice poke, kid," the catcher muttered.

"But after you get the feel of one or two, you're on your own," Applegate had said. "Oh, I may decide to amuse myself occasionally but don't get the idea you're going to be any robot. You'll be on your own."

The next one he hit into the same spot.

"Nice poke again, boy."

Something was bubbling up inside Joe, making him want to laugh, but he set his jaw, dug in his spikes.

"See what you can do with this one," Pratt called. He delivered, and then turned to watch the ball sail into deep right center.

"Hey," Joe heard a voice shouting, "somebody better go in and get Benny out here. Hold it a minute, Rocky."

Pratt stood on the mound, bouncing the ball in his glove. Joe waggled the bat, not so much as wanting to disturb the position of his feet for fear of breaking the spell.

When Mr. van Buren appeared he called, "Bear down this time, Rocky," and took a stand near the first-base coach's box.

Other activity ceased. Additional players hurried from the dressing room, and while all watched, Joe Hardy swung four times more; three were modest-length home runs, and the fourth went clear over the upper right-field stands, quite a poke in Detroit.

At this point, Mr. van Buren called a halt. "Okay, kid," he said in a restrained voice; but his grip on Joe's biceps as he steered him toward the dugout was anything but calm. At the same time he started shouting hoarsely, "Kent! Where's Kent? . . . Well, go find him, quick!"

Kent Kenyon, Joe learned in a few minutes, was the club's road secretary, the only official traveling with the team who was authorized to sign new players to a contract.

5 The next morning Joe tried to buy a Washington paper first at the hotel, but he had to walk three blocks before he found a place that sold one. It was the same paper which Bess, perhaps even at this moment, was spreading beside her plate at breakfast. But certainly not to its sports page, Joe knew. More likely to the obituary page.

It was to the sports page that he opened it immediately, and his eye ran straight off to the right-hand column. He read:

"Detroit, July 22—Two pinch-hit home runs off the bat of a 21-year-old ex-sandlotter carried the Nats to a double win over the Tigers tonight, for their first twin victory of the season. The scores were 6 to 3 and 5 to 4.

"Young Joe Hardy, signed to a Washington contract less than an hour before the curtain-raiser of the twi-night affair, produced the Frank Merriwell pokes each time in the ninth inning, driving across four runs in all."

Joe skimmed two paragraphs and came to:

"Young Hardy, about whom little is known save that he never before had played organized ball, was sent up to the plate in the first game with the score tied 3 and 3 in the ninth and two men on base. He hit a 2 and 0 pitch into the stands to give his mates the ball game.

"In the nightcap the score was again tied, this time at four apiece, when Joe was called from the dugout to swing for Bill Gregson. He responded with another home run in almost the same spot as the first.

"The double win halted, at least temporarily, the Nats' nosedive toward seventh place and moved them to within three games of the fifth-place Tigers.

"Manager Benny van Buren, highly elated over young Hardy's feats, said the young man would be in the starting lineup for tomorrow's finale with the Tigers, after which the team moves on to Chicago. Oddly enough, young Hardy says he's not particular about what position he plays. Van Buren said he has right field in mind for the redoubtable neophyte."

"Well I'll be damned, how do you like that?" Joe asked himself jubilantly. With springs in his legs, he began walking swiftly back to the hotel, constructing an imaginary telephone conversation.

"Bess," he would say, "did you see about me in the paper this morning?"

Or he would call the office and say, "Hey, did any of you guys happen to read about a certain party named Joe Hardy in this morning's paper?" And then, his voice swelling, "Well, that's me. Joe Boyd. I'm in Detroit. We'll be home to play the Yankees the end of the week and I want to see you guys out there."

Or he would clip the story and send it to Ruth and her husband in Oklahoma with a bombshell P.S.

But as he neared the hotel, his pace dragged. He could, of course, do none of these things.

In the lobby, he dropped into a chair and read again, less jubilantly, of his exploits the evening before. When he reached the phrase "redoubtable neophyte," the thrill was the same and yet . . .

Folding the paper, he went into breakfast. Something was missing. It was like being on a television program in a strange city, with no friends to watch. He was the star performer, but he was performing in a void, with nobody from his past life to applaud, unless it was a man named Applegate.

6 But in the matter of applause, no man could have been more steadfast than Applegate. From a box seat along the right-field line he applauded hoarsely all through that afternoon as Joe led the team to a twelve-to-seven victory over the Tigers in the series finale. And when the team moved to Chicago he was in his accustomed spot for all three games, the first two played by night and the last by day. Three in a row Joe and his mates won from the White Sox, giving them a winning streak of six games and moving them to within a game of collaring the fifth-place Tigers.

It was a little after nine and Joe was lying on the bed in his hotel room, replaying in retrospect that afternoon's game, when there was a light tap at the door. "Come in," he said.

The knob rattled and a familiar voice said, "I can't. It's locked."

Joe got up and opened the door. "Well, Mr. Applegate . . ." he said.

"Why don't you cut out that Mr. Applegate stuff?" his visitor asked. "Why don't you call me App? How's it going?" He was wearing now a yellow sports shirt, a Panama hat, white flannel slacks and white perforated shoes, having explained in Detroit that although he liked "that Ivy

League stuff" he had insisted on buying for Joe, he wasn't the type to wear it himself.

"Fine so far," Joe said.

Applegate tapped a newspaper that was spread out on the bed. Its banner headline said, "Rookie slams three homers as Nats maul Sox, 11-4."

"You were really pasting them this afternoon," Applegate said. Sitting on the bed, he removed his hat. With one hand he picked up the paper and with the other began fingering his hair. There was not, particularly in front, a great deal to finger. It was black hair, rather coarse, and of greater quantity in back, with a marked hiatus about three-quarters of the way forward, after which it picked up again to present a sparse growth of forelock; it was this section that Applegate was now fingering. His beard, although there was no stubble, was very heavy and blue in appearance. His eyes were small and dark, faintly arrogant, and his lips quite thin. Coarse black hair grew over his bare arms and covered the backs of his hands, even to the topmost joints of his knuckles.

"Yes sir," he said, finishing the article. "And I haven't marked today's stuff down yet, either." From his hip pocket he took out a small black notebook. Lettered in white on the front cover was the inscription, "J. H. Batting Record Book." Opening it, he made an entry. "Three more homers today," he said. "Now, let's see, that gives you eleven in six games, counting those two pinch ones. That's an average of almost two a game. And your batting average . . ."

For a while he scribbled in silence. "The way I figure it, six-forty-five," he said finally. "I notice the A.P. makes it six-forty-four, but they didn't give you the benefit of that fourth decimal place."

He put the notebook away again. "Well," he said, "I just dropped by to see if there was anything I could do. Anything you need?"

"No," Joe said. "I can't think of a thing." Rising, he turned on the other bedside lamp and then sat in an armchair by the window.

"All packed, I see," Applegate said, indicating a piece of bright yellow luggage, his own selection, standing near the door.

"Yep. We leave at ten-thirty."

"I hear they're going to turn out and meet you at the train when you get back to Washington." Applegate smiled.

"Who?"

"The fans. After all, boy, you're almost a national figure already. Certainly a civic figure."

Joe rose and stood by the window. Outside were the myriad lights of the city, the red and blue of the neon, and the street lamps marching in double lines from the hotel.

"Doesn't it make you happy?" Applegate said.

"Sure it makes me happy," Joe said, still at the window. "Only . . ."

"Only what?"

"I don't know. Nothing, I guess."

"Well now, heavens, if you're going to feel that way," Applegate began. He pulled a pack of cigarettes from the pocket of his shirt and tapped it petulantly against the edge of his hand. "If you're going to feel that way . . ." he repeated.

"I'm okay," Joe said. "I'm not complaining. Everything's fine so far."

"All right, then," Applegate said. "Here. Do you want a cigarette?"

"No, thanks." Joe turned from the window. "I will admit it's a great kick to see those balls go sailing into the stands."

"Sure it's a kick, lad," Applegate said. He lay back on the bed, hands clasped behind his neck. "And think of the pleasure you're giving poor old Benny van Buren. He's a new man. He's not admitting it just yet, but he's even started thinking about the pennant. And think of the pleasure you're giving Old Man Welch." Applegate chuckled. "What a character *he* is. Ever meet him? You know, the club owner?"

"Sure. No, I've never met him, but I've read a lot about him."

Applegate laughed again. "He's marvelous. I think they're planning a press conference when you get back. They're going to have you sign another contract for the photographers. What did they give you on that first contract?"

"Five thousand."

"Make 'em give you ten. And incidentally, speaking of contracts . . ." Applegate looked at his watch. "Listen, as long as we've got a few minutes . . . you remember we were going to talk about terms. This seems as good a time as any. Okay?"

Joe shrugged. "I guess so."

"Do you mind if I turn out the lights?" Applegate asked. "When I'm conducting official business I don't like a great deal of light."

With the room now in darkness, he sank heavily to the bed and for a while was silent, then began muttering something indistinguishable.

"What are you doing?" Joe asked.

Applegate did not answer. The muttering continued. Joe walked over again to the window and looked down at the lights. From the next room there was the sound of a coat hanger clattering to the floor.

"Okay," Applegate said finally. "Now, the first thing I want to ask you is this. You aren't still insisting on that ridiculous escape clause you were talking about, are you?"

"I sure am."

"Oh, come on, Joe, what's wrong? Don't you like your new life? Would you rather be back selling real estate with nothing to look forward to but scratching your athlete's foot at night?"

"A deal is a deal," Joe said.

Applegate sighed. "Okay, so it was a deal," he said. "All I'm trying to do is give you as much equilibrium as possible. I mean with this escape clause in the back of your mind you'll never really feel settled."

"Precisely," Joe said.

"All right, so you don't want to feel settled. Well, I'm a

man—" Applegate broke off and began groping about on the counterpane.

"What's wrong?"

"Dropped my cigarette," he said. "Here it is. So, as I say, I'm a man of my word, so we'll make it on the trial basis. I knew you wouldn't give in, but there's no harm in trying. Now then . . ."

Applegate cleared his throat. Joe noticed that his voice seemed more high-pitched than usual and unnecessarily excited.

"What I've got in mind is a contract that says something like this: You stick with me until September twenty-first. Then on September twenty-first you make your decision. If you decide you don't like it, then I'll switch you back. Okay? Fair enough?"

"That's not exactly what I had in mind," Joe said. "Suppose I want to switch back before September twenty-first? Suppose some emergency arises?"

"I'll take care of the emergencies, lad. Look, Joe, consider my position. I can't sink a lot of time and energy into something and then have you pull out before you even give it a fair trial. Look, you started July twenty-first, right? So that would make it an even two months, and that seems fair to me."

Joe pondered silently.

"Come on, Joe, what's two months out of your life? You wanted an escape clause and you got it. And whether you know it or not, lad, that's quite a concession on my part."

"Where's the contract?"

There was a rustling noise, and when Applegate turned on the lamp he held a piece of foolscap.

"Here we go," he said, spreading it. And then he did something he had done once before, when they had had lunch in Detroit—put out his cigarette by squeezing the lighted end between thumb and forefinger. Seeing the look on Joe's face, he laughed. "You could do that if you wanted to, boy. And incidentally, how do you like being so cool? You haven't felt the heat, have you?"

"No, and I must admit it's pleasant," Joe said. "It'll come in handy when we get to Washington." He bent over the foolscap and read carefully. "You sure there's no invisible ink anywhere?"

"I don't like to hear you say things like that, Joe," Applegate said in a hurt voice.

"Okay. Now wait a minute. This says that on September twenty-first I have the privilege of switching back, but not after the twenty-first. That means that if I want to switch back on October first, for instance, I won't be able to, is that right?"

"Of course, Joe. That's what we've been saying all along."

Joe silently read further and then said, "Okay, you got a pen?"

"Sure." Applegate produced a ball point and Joe signed, then dropped into the chair again. "I'm afraid this is a bad investment for you, App. There's no chance in the world that I'll stick on after the twenty-first."

"Well . . ." Applegate lit another cigarette and sat

on the bed, looking down and trying to conceal, Joe realized, what was certainly a smirk.

Again, as on that first night, he felt a chill premonition, but he laughed and said, "You think you've got me, don't you?"

"No," Applegate said. Looking up, trying without success to regain a straight face, he said, "Not necessarily."

"Listen, App, don't sell me short. I haven't been a real-estate man for nothing."

"You were actually a very scrupulous one," Applegate said. "The file shows it . . . well, anyway, what I wanted to tell you is this. Even though you're not signed, sealed and delivered on a permanent basis yet, I'd appreciate anything you could do for us along the way.

"Like what?"

"Oh, you know . . . a word or a phrase in the right place."

"About what?"

"Oh, tell everybody what a grand thing TV is and how it's a good idea to trade in your old car on a new one every year. You know the kind of thing I mean."

Joe nodded, smiling. "I'll try to remember."

"Well," Applegate said, looking at his watch again, "I guess you don't have much time left now, and before you go to the station there's somebody I want you to meet."

"Let me ask you something first," Joe said. "What's the idea, anyway?"

"What idea?"

"I mean, why do you go around trying to suck people in on deals like this? I've been doing some thinking about you."

"Joe, I thought you wanted to be a baseball player. All your life you've wanted to be a baseball player."

"Wait a minute. Let me put it another way. I mean, why do you want people down there in the first place?"

"That's a common fallacy," Applegate said. "It's not necessarily down anywhere."

"What's it like there, anyway?"

"It's different things to different people," Applegate said. "I'll tell you about it some time."

"Okay. Well, to get back to what I was asking, though . . . why do you want to see all these people go wherever it is? Is it because misery loves company?"

Crushing his cigarette, Applegate looked at him narrowly. "Who's miserable?" he said, and rose. "Come on, I'll go into that with you some other time. Right now I want you to meet this girl. She's enough to knock your eyeballs back against your cerebellum."

"A girl? Listen, you know I'm married."

"So who said you weren't? You don't have to take advantage of this if you don't want to, but—as far as that goes . . ." And Applegate's voice trailed off.

"What's that?"

"I said into each life a little strange fruit must fall, and what nobody don't know won't hurt 'em. Come on, let's get your stuff downstairs. It's almost time for you to leave."

She was sitting in the lobby, near the cigar stand, and as Joe and Applegate approached she glanced up from a newspaper, uncrossed her knees and smiled.

"Joe, this is Lola," Applegate said.

"Hello, Lola."

"How do you do, Mr. Hardy?" She held out her hand.

"Lola is the most beautiful girl in the world," Applegate said, not with the rising inflection that might be expected in such a statement, but simply as a pronouncement of fact.

And Joe did not doubt it. His glance fell before hers, fell to her black linen pumps and her slim ankles, then reached again for her eyes. They were dark; he had an impression of lavender. She wore a black dress, off both tanned shoulders, and her hair was as black as her dress. It was short hair and at first glance might have been considered haphazardly cut, but looking again Joe realized there was a pattern to its tousle.

"You'll be seeing a lot of Lola," Applegate said. "Excuse me, I want to get a cigar."

"I've just been reading about you, Mr. Hardy," the girl said, recrossing her legs.

"Really?" Joe said uneasily.

"You must be a superlative ball player." Her voice was soft and cultured.

"It's a lot of fun," he said. There were no other chairs near and he sat on his suitcase but felt awkward and got up again.

"I would simply adore to watch you some time," Lola said. "What city is it you go to now?"

"Washington," Joe said.

Across the lobby he saw some of the team heading for the street. A bell boy was approaching him. "The team's about to leave, Mr. Hardy," he said.

"Oh. Okay." Joe stood aside to let the bell boy pick up his bag. "I'm afraid I'll have to leave now," he said.

"Well, it was so nice meeting you, Mr. Hardy." The girl again held out her hand. Her arm was slim, her shoulder sleek. "Perhaps I shall be seeing you in Washington some time, yes?"

"That would be fine," Joe said. "Well, good-bye."

As he started off after the bell boy, he remembered to look around for Applegate, but Applegate was nowhere to be seen.

7 "Now let me get this straight, Joe. If you've never played organized ball before, where did you learn to hit like that?"

It seemed to Joe, as he stood there facing the reporters and photographers, that he had daydreamed a scene like this while mowing the lawn one summer. Some summer. This, and the scene early that morning when the crowd had met the train, a crowd that had eyes mostly for Joe Hardy.

"Well," he replied carefully, modestly, "It just came naturally to me, I guess."

The news conference was being held in the ball-park office. Joe stood backed against a round walnut table and behind him, seated about the table, were Mr. Adam Welch, the club's nonagenarian owner; a smiling Mr. van Buren, and other club officials and hangers-on. The discarded traces of a pinochle game lay on the table. Photographs of greats and near-greats out of the team's past lined the walls.

"Now wait a minute, Joe. You're not telling us that out in Detroit was the first time you ever swung a bat, are you?" a second reporter demanded. There were about twelve in all, including four from New York papers, in town for the three-game series with the Yankees, which would begin the following night.

"Oh, no, of course not," Joe said. "I've played quite a bit of sandlot ball."

"Sandlot ball!" one of the reporters bellowed. A couple of radio men were recording the conference on tape, and the red light on their recording machine winced at the volume. "You mean you came straight off the sandlots and hit the ball over the right-field stands in Detroit? And averaged almost two homers a game ever since?"

"Yes, that's right," Joe said. He looked at his feet, feeling something very much like guilt. He had never been good at lying, and this was lying in public, although on the other hand the press conference hadn't been his idea.

Looking up again, he saw a familiar figure enter the room and casually take a stand at the outer fringe of reporters. Familiar and yet different today. Applegate looked quite natty. He had discarded the yellow sports shirt and now wore a gray suit with a pearl gray snap-brim hat. Catching Joe's eye, he winked and held up his thumb and forefinger in a circle. Involuntarily, Joe found his presence comforting.

"Well, we'll let that one pass, Joe," the reporter said. "We'll take your word for it. Now tell us something about yourself. Are you married?"

Joe hesitated, then saw Applegate shake his head vigorously.

"No," he said.

"What do you do for a living?"

"What does he do for a living!" Behind him, Joe heard Mr. Welch's piping voice scornfully repeat the question and then chortle. "What do you think this is if it's not a living?" Mr. Welch demanded, flapping a newly drawn contract.

Joe laughed. "I hope it's going to be baseball," he said.

"Before this, I mean," the reporter said with some exasperation.

"Oh, well, odd jobs. Carpenter's helper. A little farm work."

"Where you from, Joe?"

"My home town is in Missouri."

"What town is that?"

Joe hesitated. "Hannibal," he said.

"You mean where Mark Twain came from?"

"That's right."

All the reporters scribbled industriously at this point, and one of them said, "Tom Sawyer makes good in the big leagues."

"Tell us your favorite food, Mr. Hardy," a voice boomed, and it was Applegate, who himself now had a pencil in hand and was writing on the back of an envelope. The reporters turned. "Who's that—Injun Joe?" one of them muttered.

"Steak, I guess," Joe Hardy said. All except Applegate and one reporter let this pass, and the reporter immediately and impatiently scribbled through his notation, saying in a victimized tone, "What the hell."

"Say, listen, Joe—listen Benny—I wonder if we could get that picture of Joe signing now," one of the photographers asked. "It's getting late."

"Sure." Mr. van Buren swept the pinochle deck together and set it on a massive desk, next to a block of polished wood on which the name Adam Welch was carved.

"Now, how about Joe in the middle, signing the new contract, and Mr. Welch, you on one side and be tearing up the old one, and Benny, you on the other side and just kind of looking happy, or something."

Mr. van Buren smiled. "I *am* happy," he said.

Mr. Welch walked around to the spot assigned, a slight figure of a man, moving with short, shuffling steps but with shoulders back and his body held very erect in the three-button banker's gray suit.

Joe seated himself and picked up a fountain pen, his eye drawn by the figures $10,000 on the third line. "I appreciate this, Mr. Welch," he said, feeling a strong fondness for the old man, and it was a fondness that had existed long before this, a fondness that had nothing to do with the ten thousand dollars. Even though he knew him only from newspaper references, he felt that he knew him intimately and for years had admired him for his spirit, his hope, his hatred of the Yankees.

"Glad to do it, boy," the old man said, then piped excitedly, "Wait a minute, where's my pillow? Somebody get me my pillow."

A pillow was obtained from the swivel chair behind his desk, and he now reached a more respectable height above the table, high enough so that he could comfortably rest his forearms on its surface, showing heavily veined hands and the impeccably pressed sleeves of his jacket. His thick white hair was carefully parted on the side, and a magnificent snow-white goatee adorned his chin. His eyes were watery blue, but very alert and excited now, as he held the contract aloft. Flash bulbs blinked as he tore it down the middle, and as Joe signed the new one, and as Benny van Buren smiled benignly.

"Good," a photographer said. "Now once more. Mr. Welch, you make out like you're tearing it some more," and the flash bulbs blinked again.

With the photographers gone, and with Joe and Mr. Welch and Mr. van Buren still seated at the table, one of the reporters asked, "Now Mr. Hardy, before we break it up, there's just one question I'd like to ask. How is it that you decided to latch onto a team like the Senators?"

"Why not?" Joe asked, nettled.

"Why didn't you try to hook up with the Yankee system, or one of the good National League clubs instead?"

"I wouldn't call that exactly a tactful question," Joe said. In the back of the room, he saw Applegate smile fleetingly, then put away his pencil and leave.

"Perhaps not tactful but pertinent," the reporter said.

Mr. Welch's eyes were blinking excitedly beneath the carefully brushed white brows. "What's your name, young fellow?" he asked the reporter.

Removing a white pipe with a curved stem from his mouth, the offender answered coolly, "Head. Luster Head."

"You must be new around here, aren't you?" Mr. Welch asked, standing now, beginning to tremble slightly.

"Around here, yes," the reporter replied drily. "It's been some time since I covered a press conference involving the Washington Senators."

"What's your paper, young fellow?" Mr. Welch demanded.

"The New York *Bugle.*"

From the corner of his eye, Joe saw Mr. van Buren making frantic gesticulations. One of the local reporters, picking up the cue, asked in a soothing voice, "Mr. Welch, with Joe Hardy on the club, you'll probably win the pennant in a breeze, right?"

"I should think so," the old man said, and, mollified, sank back onto his pillow again, but was immediately up as the reporter named Head sniffed and said, "You mean you think you're going to beat the Yankees?"

"Beat the Yankees!" Mr. Welch was shaking a gnarled forefinger at Head. "You can bet your sweet life we'll beat the Yankees. What makes you think we won't beat the Yankees, young man?"

"Now take it easy, Mr. Welch," one of his pinochle colleagues said. "Don't get excited."

"I just want this young fellow to answer me that one question," Mr. Welch said, his usually high thin voice breaking at the end of the sentence into a phlegmy rattle.

Joe looked at him with compassion, then glared at the reporter.

"Come on, Mr. Welch, don't get excited," Mr. van Buren said, laying a hand on his shoulder. "Just take it easy now."

Head smiled tolerantly. "Okay, Mr. Welch, you're going to beat the Yankees. You're going to win the pennant by twenty-nine games. I'm sorry."

Joe felt an urge to rush Head and swing, but restrained it. It was more than likely that Applegate was responsible for this . . . the knowing smile as he left. And if it was Applegate's doing, where was the motive, unless just pure malice?

Mr. Welch was regarding Head suspiciously, still weaving behind the table. "Don't get sarcastic, young fellow," he said.

"Well, twenty-eight games then," Head said.

"Why, you listen to me, young man," Mr. Welch said, enraged. "If it wasn't for just blind devil's luck those Yankees would have dropped clear out of the League by now. They'd be down—"

Somebody handed him a cup of water, and he sipped it, never taking his eyes from the offending reporter.

". . . down in the Three-Eye League by now, that's where they'd be," he managed, and then began to grope for his collar button, pulling loose his tie from the round stiff collar. Hands grasped his shoulders and pressed him gently back onto his pillow, where he sat, breathing heavily, eyes watering, but still glaring defiantly at Head.

"All right, fellows, I guess we'd better break it up now," Mr. van Buren said. "And next time we'll just skip any questions about the Yankees, okay?"

Head sucked thoughtfully at his pipe. His face was smooth and white, well cared for. He wore a wrist watch with a gold band. "I'm sorry, Ben, I wasn't aware of your house rules," he said. Walking calmly over to the table, he knocked the pipe against an ash tray and asked, "But do you honestly mean to tell me that Mr. Welch doesn't realize the Yankees have won the pennant the past nine years?"

Mr. van Buren glanced nervously back at Mr. Welch, but the old man was sitting with glazed eyes now and seemed not to hear.

"Each year he thinks we're going to lick the Yankees and he keeps on thinking it right up until the end of the season," Mr. van Buren said. "But the point is, don't ever mention Yankees around him again. It upsets him."

"Well, I won't be around to give you any trouble any more," Head said, putting his pen away. "I wouldn't have been here today if the paper hadn't decided to cover the young hot shot here. Anyway, I apologize."

The reporters headed for the door and then stopped, arrested by the sound of a weak, piping voice.

"Wait a minute," Mr. Welch said, and then, clearing his throat, "Wait just a minute, I've got something I want to say."

Joe turned and was touched at the transformation. Mr. Welch's shoulders had sagged. His face was not the happy, excited face it had been early in the news conference; nor was it angry, as it had been a few minutes before. It was now the humble face of a very old man.

The reporters stood attentive. Mr. Welch rose slowly, fingering a worn gold watch fob that hung from a pocket of his vest.

"I just want to answer that young fellow's question," he said. Then, raising his head, he looked steadfastly at each reporter in turn. "He wanted to know if I realized the Yankees had won the pennant so many years, and whether I realized we were always out of it."

He paused, and a look of infinite sadness came over the aged face.

"The answer is yes. I know it. I know both those things."

Among the reporters, feet shuffled in embarrassment.

"I know you fellows think I'm a crazy old fool," Mr. Welch went on, "but when you get to be an old man, sometimes you can't help it. Especially when there's something inside that makes you keep on hoping. So that's . . ."

But he broke off and sat down, bending his head low over folded hands. There was a hush in the room, broken finally by Head, who said softly, "Sorry again, Ben," and headed for the door.

The others followed, but one of them turned and asked in a subdued voice, "Incidentally, Ben, are you still going to let Roscoe Ent pitch against the Athletics this weekend? I meant to ask you earlier."

"No," Mr. van Buren said. "Of course not." He paused and his jaw set. "You can put this down if you like, boys. From now on we're going out on that field fully expecting to win every game we play. We've got our eye on that pennant. We're not thinking in terms of being three or four or six or eight games out of the first division. We're thinking in terms of how many games we're out of first place. Right, Mr. Welch?"

The old man was being led from the room. Smiling sadly, he nodded, "Right, Benny," he said.

"Right, Joe?" Mr. van Buren clapped Joe on the shoulder.

"I don't see why not, Ben," Joe replied.

"Thatta boy, and congratulations on your new contract."

A refrain began pulsing through Joe's head. "Win one for the Gipper," it ran, and then was changed to "Win one for Mr. Welch."

It lasted until, leaving the office a few minutes later, he noticed a figure dart around the corner of the building. After a short distance, he looked back and saw a man no taller than Mr. Welch but many years younger, glaring after him. There was anger on the man's face and his lips were moving. Joe turned and walked on, puzzled until it came to him that the man must, of course, have been Roscoe Ent, and although he hadn't thought about it before, Roscoe Ent had cause to hate Joe Hardy. He looked back again, but Ent had disappeared.

8 Roscoe Ent, a clown and an occasional pitcher, had been signed on by the club as an attendance booster a number of years before, when the fans, depressed by the team's chronic seventh-place-itis, began to stay away from the park in large numbers.

It was ironic, Joe thought, walking on, that he should be hated by Roscoe Ent. Because even though Ent was a symbol of the team's mediocrity, Joe had developed a genuine liking for the little fellow during seasons past.

Roscoe never made the road trips, but when the team was home he was always there in his natty little uniform, a full-fledged and very proud member of the squad. Sometimes in the ninth, with the team far behind, he was permitted to pitch. He could get the ball over the plate and he had a tiny curve, but most of the time he was hit hard. But the laws of chance that govern falling baseballs usually limited the damage. Beyond his occasional pitching stints, he put on a little show at every game—a few dance steps; playing various tricks on his teammates; driving a midget car around the infield and stopping to walk over on his hands and touch each base. The fans loved it, and, largely because of Roscoe, attendance remained at respectable levels no matter how mediocre the caliber of the team's play.

As Joe passed by, there were long lines at the ticket windows. People buying tickets for tomorrow night and for the other games of the Yankee series. He had heard somebody say the advance sale was the largest in twenty years. The attraction: Joe Hardy.

Roscoe Ent, he realized, saw the handwriting on the wall. A fired-up team playing good ball would need no attendance booster, would certainly not permit a comedian to pitch regardless of the score. It was Joe Hardy who had fired up the team. It was Joe Hardy who might cost him his job.

And how does that make you feel, Joe asked himself. Poor Roscoe. And yet he couldn't blame himself. He had done no evil greater than help the team win, and winning after all was theoretically the team's ambition.

Furthermore, he had on his mind something more important than Roscoe Ent. A decision to make.

Reaching the boulevard beyond the ball-park grounds, he paused and looked off to the right, following with his eye the long stretch of trolley line winding northward into the distance.

A decision he had been mulling ever since the team had arrived from Chicago that morning.

A trolley was approaching, was coming now to a stop just before him, but when he made no move the motorman picked up speed again. He stood there on the sidewalk, looking after it.

Still undecided, he went into a drug store and ordered a root beer, sat sipping it slowly, looking at himself in the mirror behind the soda fountain. It was still a surprise to see this face and, he admitted, still a pleasure. He sighed. The ideal thing, of course, even a solution of sorts, would be if Bess too could have . . . But Bess would have no part of Applegate. She would have driven him off with a broomstick. Bess . . .

Leaving the root beer unfinished, he strode out resolutely and this time boarded the trolley. At least he could see that she was all right.

She was in the yard. Walking up the hill, he saw her from half a block away, bending near the side border, stout but neat in the light blue dress she often wore for gardening. As he reached the crest of the hill, she rose and brushed back her hair, then, glancing in his direction, knelt again beside her flower bed. At this moment, he knew, she was puzzled and curious, because she prided herself on knowing everybody in the neighborhood. He slowed his pace, eyes on the gray head bent so intently. She was loosening the dirt around the flowers, in fact around a rose bush that he had planted for her that spring. She had been very tender with that rose bush. At night, he knew, she sneaked out to water it, like Old Man Everett with his azaleas.

When he came to a stop, she looked up again, this time full at him, with no sign of recognition. He was moved by the age in her face. Just in these few days it seemed much older. It was, he thought, like watching a child grow taller. When you grow old with a person, see her day by day, you don't notice; but now, with the sense of his own youth . . .

Yet, he certainly couldn't say that her face showed anxiety or any particular sense of loss. It seemed, in fact, quite serene.

"Oh, Mr. Hardy."

He hadn't heard the car approach; or at least he had been too intent to notice. But it was already at the curb, a green convertible, long, rakish, and of no recognizable make, and she was fluttering her hand at him.

"Why, hello . . . hello, Lola."

Bess looked up curiously and for a moment he was afraid she had recognized his voice, even though it was not his own. But she was picking up the bushel basket she used for weeds and walking toward the back yard, then putting it down and hurrying into the house, for the telephone was ringing.

Joe turned to Lola, his eye drawn by the long, graceful line of her tanned neck. She wore a green striped blouse of men's shirting, unbuttoned at the throat.

"I was hoping I might run across you, Mr. Hardy," she said.

He walked over to the car, looking furtively toward the house. Lola was another woman, and an attractive one. The habits of long years were hard to break.

"I was wondering if you would do me a favor," she said. One hand rested lightly on the wheel. She was gazing at him from the dark clear eyes; her lips were slightly parted, her complexion tanned and smooth, unmarred even by the humidity.

"I thought you were in Chicago," he said.

"Yes, I was," she said, turning the ignition key, "but now I'm here. Come on, hop in."

Whether it was the glib way she spoke of distances or something else, he was convinced at that moment that the telephone call was from Applegate. He pictured Applegate in some telephone booth, hanging up when Bess answered.

But Bess had not come out again, and maybe Applegate had not hung up. Maybe they were having a long conversation. Maybe Applegate was posing as an antique dealer.

Applegate was very resourceful.

Joe smiled. But Applegate and Lola had gone to a lot of unnecessary trouble. He hadn't intended speaking to Bess. He had just wanted to see her.

"Okay," he said, and with a final look toward the house he got into the car. "What can I do for you?"

Before answering, Lola shifted and raced off down the street. They had gone two blocks when she said, "Well, I wanted to see Mount Vernon, and I thought maybe you would be kind enough to show me the way."

"Mount Vernon?" He laughed.

"What's wrong with that?" she asked, her eyes wide in innocence. And her eyes, he had to admit, were incredible. A deep lavender, with rich dark lashes looking as soft as a cashmere sweater.

"It's just that you don't seem the type to visit Mount Vernon," he said.

"Oh, but I hear it is very interesting," she said. "I've been told that it is one of the most beautiful places in the country. A garden spot, really . . ."

Joe looked at her quizzically, and then with reluctant admiration, as his eyes moved to the smooth even tan of her slim arms, the gracefully shaped hands gripping the wheel. She drove easily, with no trace of the tension he had always associated with women drivers.

But then he laughed again. "Mount Vernon! It seems to me that you and Applegate between you could have thought up something better than that."

"Why, Mr. Hardy . . ." Her voice and eyes indicated genuine hurt, and he checked himself. Maybe he had jumped to a conclusion. Suppose this girl was not Applegate's minion? Suppose, for instance, she was just a prospect, as he himself once had been a prospect?

But this, of course, was inconceivable.

"How long have you known Applegate?" he asked, watching her face.

"Oh, a year or so."

"What do you think of him?"

"Mr. Applegate? Well, I think he's a very dynamic person . . . he has a lot of drive . . ."

For just a second, Joe felt puzzled. But after all, she had driven to his house, obviously straight as an arrow, arriving at what Applegate would have considered a critical moment. Hadn't Applegate made a remark once about emergency calls? To remember these things was to puzzle no longer.

As she drove, he studied the slender, childlike grace of her neck. She could be no more than 20, younger even than Joe's daughter Ruth.

The poor kid.

"Which way do I go, Mr. Hardy?"

"Don't tell me you're still thinking about Mount Vernon," he said.

"But of course," she said, and her voice sounded disappointed.

"Oh now, come on, Lola. Let's get serious."

"But I am serious. Terribly serious. You promised."

"Well," Joe said, "even if you are serious, which I doubt, I'm afraid it's too late to go there today. It's quite a distance, and we'd never make it before closing time. If you really want to go, maybe I can take you some other day."

"Would you, Joe?" Her look was grateful and something more, and the paternal feeling of a few seconds before suddenly went up in smoke. In its place he felt a deep disturbance. He tried to remember how many years it had been since a woman had spoken his name like that, looked at him like that.

"Yes," he said. "Maybe. Listen, I guess I'd better be getting back to the hotel."

Uneasily he lit a cigarette. Something deeply significant was happening, and as nearly as he could analyze, it had something to do with a war between Joe Boyd and Joe Hardy.

"Is there any possibility that we could have dinner together?" Lola said. She was speaking now with the trace of an accent. He had noticed it several times before. At other times it was not present.

"No, I'm afraid not," Joe said.

"I'm so sorry," she said. "Well, I'll be seeing you at the ball park tomorrow night, anyway. I will be out there always."

"That's very flattering," Joe said.

"Mr. Applegate says you are poetry in motion."

"Does he?" Joe said absently.

"Absolute poetry."

"Could you drop me at the hotel?" he said. "Or is it out of your way?"

"Not in the slightest," she said. "Yes, I will drop you, reluctantly."

But traffic became progressively heavier, and they were still many blocks from the hotel when it was blocked altogether. When Joe looked, the line of cars ahead seemed endless.

Lola settled back in the seat.

"Far as you can see," Joe said, craning his neck. "This is terrible."

"Oh, Joe, it's not so bad." Lola stretched, and the green blouse went tight. "It's probably just some minor accident. I'm sure it will clear up soon, and then everyone will spin along home." She smiled. "Cars are such fun, don't you think? I've only been driving for a year or so, and I've never really enjoyed anything so much."

The car ahead moved up a foot and the car behind

sounded its horn. Obediently, Lola closed the gap.

"I'll bet we haven't gone ten feet since we got here," Joe said.

"I know," she said, smiling. "Look at the poor things."

Drivers with faces greasy and tired from the long day's humidity were looking angrily out of windows, some forward and some backward.

But Joe was not looking at them. He was looking at Lola, thinking that she was a remarkable combination of slender and buxom, and the disturbance this time was violent.

She had noticed. Smiling slowly, she said, "Are you sure you can't have dinner with me, Joe?" And then she said, "Joe! Where are you going?"

He had already slammed the door and stood now with his hand on the sill. "I'm sorry to run out on you like this," he said, "but I really am in a hurry."

Without waiting for her to reply, he walked between cars to the curb, deeply shaken. It's one thing to set out to redeem a baseball team, he told himself sternly, but quite another to feel the way you were just feeling about another woman.

As he reached the sidewalk, he turned, expecting to see a smirk, to see mirthful disdain, or even not to see her at all. But she was looking after him with an expression of reproach, of genuine hurt. He waved, but she did not wave back and now her face changed. She seemed to be looking beyond him, finding something that brought her great sadness.

	The night of the game was clear and warm.
9	Long before game time, crowds began
	moving on the ball park, moving from all
	directions toward the light towers, the giant

beacons rearing high above the grandstand and casting a
brilliance visible for blocks around. By ones and twos and in
voluble, excited groups they came, pausing only to buy a
scorecard and moving on then up the ramp, anticipatory,
already feeling the special quality that had drawn them,
for this was the night that Joe Hardy would meet the peer-
less monsters head on.

It was three-quarters of an hour before game time and
the stands were already almost full when Joe came face to
face with Roscoe Ent.

Joe had finished batting practice and was heading for
the water cooler when he chanced to look toward right
field and there saw the little man, dressed in his Washington uniform, doing a few dance steps near the foul line.
From the fans in the vicinity there came only a smattering
of laughter, and as Joe watched, Ent broke off abruptly and
took a seat on the railing in front of the right-field boxes.

Struck by sympathy, Joe by-passed the dugout and
headed for right field. A long ripple of applause preceded

him, reaching all the way into the right-field corner. Doff-ing his cap in acknowledgment to the fans, and waving for the second time that night to Applegate and Lola, who had been in their box seats since seven-thirty, Joe walked up to Ent and said, "I don't believe I've met you. My name is Hardy."

He was regarded without enthusiasm. "Yeah, I know," was the sour reply.

Undaunted, Joe said pleasantly, "You're Roscoe Ent, aren't you?"

"How'd you guess it?" Ent said sarcastically, giving the long peak of his blue cap a savage tug.

Making no attempt to conceal his distaste for Joe's prox-imity, he slid two or three feet away along the railing. Then he glared up into the stands where a fan with a loud, hoarse voice had just shouted something about a bus. As Ent turned, Joe noticed that he wore the numeral 13 on the back of his uniform.

"How's it going?" Joe asked.

"What do *you* think, buster?" Ent said.

"It's end of the line for you, Ent," the fan shouted. "You might as well go buy your bus ticket."

Applegate, Joe could see, was smiling appreciatively at the byplay between Ent and the raucous fan, looking ex-pectantly from one to the other.

"It won't be long now, Ent," the fan yelled.

Tight-lipped, the little man did not turn this time but sat staring off in the direction of the left-field bleachers.

Then, noticing Joe's appraising look, he said with heavy

sarcasm, "Yeah, I know. I don't look like a pitcher. Go ahead and tell me."

"I wasn't thinking that," Joe said civilly. "After all, who's to say what a pitcher is supposed to look like?"

"You must be a philosopher," Ent said.

"Why don't you go pitch for the rinkydinks, Ent?" the fan shouted.

Ent rose and stood looking dolefully toward the outfield. He was, Joe estimated, about five feet tall; certainly no more, and yet the little body was stocky and well proportioned. The small uniform fitted him perfectly, quite nattily, and the spiked shoes on the stubby feet were shined to a high luster. Only the peak of the cap seemed outsize. Standing now with a hand in his hip pocket, he might have been a bat boy; yet his face was mature, lined and heavily seamed around the mouth and jowls, and looking now quite dour.

"Back to Pocomoke for you, Ent," the fan bellowed.

Joe winced. When the Applegates scurry about disturbing the status quo, it is the Roscoe Ents of the world who suffer. The fans who scoffed tonight were the same fans who had applauded during the team's last home stand. Wanting to speak a word of comfort, Joe could find nothing to say.

Hands on hips, Ent glared again back into the stands, then turned and began walking slowly across the foul line in direction of the center-field bullpen.

"See you later, Roscoe," Joe said.

Ent didn't answer, didn't even turn, merely made a

shooing motion in Joe's direction with his gloved hand and continued slowly and dejectedly toward the bullpen.

Joe sighed and scuffed the grass.

"Hey, Joe."

Applegate, back again to his yellow sports shirt and Panama hat, waved a half-eaten frankfurter and roll. He seemed to have one in his hand every time Joe looked in his direction.

"You still eating?" Joe asked.

"I didn't have much dinner. Listen, what's that Ent giving you?"

Lola sat starched and prim in a white dress. Not once had she met his eyes, and when he looked at her now she examined her scorecard. "There's a rule, isn't there, Mr. Applegate," she said, head still lowered, "that says a player can be fined for talking to the spectators?"

"Oh, well, if he's fined I'll pay for it," said Applegate, waving his frankfurter expansively. "What's the point of coming out to a game, if you can't have a few words with your friends? So what's with this Ent, Joe?"

"Oh, nothing. I feel sorry for him."

"Well, don't take anything off him," Applegate said, and then with irritation wiped at his shirt front. "Lousy mustard. . . . It's a good thing I've got this shirt on," he went on more cheerfully. "It won't even show. Well, let 'em have it, boy. This is the night."

It has been written that when the Yankees took the field in that decade of the 1950's, they must have appeared

· 82 ·

seven feet tall to the opposing team and, to the opposing pitcher, even taller when they strode to the plate.

Hailed again by applause, Joe retraced his steps from right field and paused near the coach's box to watch them at infield practice. Forgetting Ent for the moment, he felt a pulse of anticipation, thought again of all the years he had regarded these gray-uniformed robots as objects of hate. Yet now they looked quite ordinary: highly adept and graceful as they whipped the ball about the infield, true, but still no more than human.

The Yankee first baseman turned his head. "Hiya, Joe," he said pleasantly. "You gonna hit a couple tonight?"

In character as always; meticulous, as always, never to patronize or belittle the opposing team. It was subtle and insidious. It could be lulling. They courted you with good fellowship and then beat your brains out.

Not answering, Joe turned back toward the dugout, and his eye was caught by two kids, boys of about ten, sitting in a box. They were twins, towheads. Solemnly deadpan, obviously unlulled, they were chanting, "Yang-kees sti-ink; Yang-kees sti-ink, stoopid owuld Yang-kees."

Catching sight of Joe, they jumped up and said variously, "Thatta boy, Joe! Hit a homer tonight, Joe! Gonna beat those stinkers tonight, aren't we, Joe?"

He waved to them and then to Mr. Welch, who had his habitual seat next to the team's dugout. His face was ruddy and his eyes excited above the lapels of his gabardine topcoat, upturned to keep the night air from his throat and chest, although the air this night was very mild. "Put it on em, Joe, boy," the old man shouted, and his voice and manner now were anything but resigned. "Put it on 'em."

Joe paused for a moment at the head of the dugout steps. The towheads were standing now, holding their noses and booing the maneuvers of the Yankee infield. Then he heard Mr. van Buren say, "All right, team, everybody down in the dressing room," and he said it with the mien and tone of a football coach about to give a pep talk.

Mr. van Buren was backed against the bulletin board. "Everybody here?" he asked. "Okay." Whereupon he took something from his hip pocket; when he held it up, Joe saw that it was a newspaper clipping. "This is a column called 'Heading In' by a guy named Head who writes for the New York *Bugle*," Mr. van Buren said. "This is what he wrote this morning. I don't have to read the whole thing to you. Just these two sentences."

Clearing his throat, he looked about the room and read: "They'd have you believe down here in Washington that the ball club has a new spirit. Interesting if true, but our own hunch is that, regrettably for both themselves and the rest of the league, they're still the same old slipshod, never-say-win Senators."

As Mr. van Buren finished reading, there was at first deep electric silence, broken quickly by imprecations, by name calling, threats, and resolutions; then the clatter of many spiked shoes moving across the concrete floor, heading toward the steps of the dugout, to the field, to battle with the Yankees, vaunted prides of Luster Head and others.

But it was not for nothing, Joe was quick to admit, that they wore the word YANKEES across their shirt fronts. This was not their first encounter with a hopped-up team. The Chicago White Sox had been hopped up, to no avail, for years. Unperturbed, and with cold, seemingly mechanical exactitude, they went about the business of winning another ball game. Willie Todd, the wily southpaw, was pitching for the Yankees that night and Willie was on. His placid, moonlike face never changing expression, he bent his assortment of slow curves and sliders over the corners with such precision that the Senators seldom got solid wood on the ball. His first two trips to the plate, even Joe was stopped. One ball he hit on a screeching line toward right center, but it was snared by the Yankee center fielder on an incredible stab; another he hit in a high arc to the base of the left-center bleacher wall, but the Yankee left fielder, playing deep and shading toward right, had plenty of time to get there.

But if Willie Todd was on that night, so too was Sammy Ransom, the Senators' raw-boned fireballer, and when Joe Hardy came up for his third trip with two out in the seventh inning, the score was knotted at nothing-nothing. With the pleas of forty thousand fans ringing through the big park, Joe went to a three-one count and then lashed a soaring liner toward right field. It spelled home run the second it left his bat, and as the ball disappeared behind the wall the sound that rang out was near deafening. Slowly Joe Hardy completed the circuit, taking outstretched hands as he crossed the plate, doffing his cap as he walked to the dugout, and looking toward the right-field boxes. Lola sat immobile now, but as he had crossed first base on the way around, he had seen her swatting Applegate rapturously over the head with her scorecard.

In the eighth the Yankees went down in order, but in the ninth the gallant Ransom faltered. Obviously tired, and with the hop gone from his fast ball, Sammy walked the first batter. The second hit into a fast double play, but Sammy, reprieved and with the game now in his hip pocket, walked the next man on four pitches. That brought up Will Talliaferro, the Yankees' hard-hitting second sacker.

The stands were silent as Sammy reared back and fogged in the first one for a strike.

From his position in right field, Joe groaned. Sammy was trying to throw it past the batter when his steam was gone. Work on him, Joe silently cautioned the beleaguered pitcher. Fool him. Don't throw him fast balls.

Bent from the waist, hands on knees, Joe waited. Sammy threw, and Joe saw the umpire's right hand go up even before the sound of "Strike tuh" reached his ears. He stood again, easing the tension. It was Talliaferro who was in the hole now. Ransom walked back to the resin bag, picked it up, dropped it, peered in for his signal. The Yankee runner led warily off first. The stands grew hushed, and Joe again bent forward, hands on his knees.

Crack!

He saw the ball only as a streak of white, rising above the first baseman's head, hugging the foul line; saw the gray uniform of the baserunner blurring toward second, and then he had turned his back and was racing for the right-field stands. Only from the corner of his right eye did he see the ball reaching the spot before he reached the spot —or not quite before, because Joe had thrown up his gloved hand and taken the ball just as it was dropping over the barrier.

And then, carrying the ball, he was jogging toward the infield; and the fans, shocked at first into silence, were on their feet now, shouting the name of Joe Hardy.

| 10 | While the opener of the Yankee series had been hard fought, in the two games that followed the Senators clobbered the champions with relative ease, winning ten to four

and fourteen to eight. In the second game, Joe contributed two home runs, and in the third game another, this last a titanic clout over the wall in dead center, a feat accomplished previously only by the Messrs. Ruth, Gehrig, and Larry Doby, although surpassed in a somewhat different direction back in 1953 by the veteran Mickey Mantle, then of the Yankees and currently of the Cleveland Indians.

Triumphantly, the team then journeyed to New York to meet the same Yankees in a two-game series which began a swing around the East. Again they took the measure of the by-then very edgy champions, this time by scores of six to one and eleven to nine, and these were consecutive victories ten and eleven in the streak that had begun the evening of Joe's arrival in Detroit.

The Tigers had been collared during the Yankee series in Washington, and with the second victory in New York, Joe and his mates slipped half a game ahead of the Indians, so that when they boarded the train for Boston it was as members of the first division. Only an elderly clubhouse custodian, Mr. Welch, and Joe Boyd remembered a time when the Senators had been so high in the race so late in the season. They were now only five games behind the White Sox who, in the interim, had sunk to third, supplanted by the ebullient Baltimore Orioles.

Although both Joe and the team for days had been subjects of rabid interest in the public press, it was during the series in Boston that the sports writers made a truly concerted rush for the bandwagon. Columnist after columnist began to speculate that the 1958 Washington Senators might just possibly emulate the storied Boston Braves of 1914 who, mired in last place on July 4 of that year, climbed out to the pennant. And Joe, after hitting three home runs in the first game of the Boston series, picked up the paper next morning to find one columnist suggesting that even though he never played another game he should be given a place in the Hall of Fame at Cooperstown, simply on the basis of what he had already achieved. While others did not go so far, they clearly believed there might come a day when Ty Cobb, Babe Ruth, and others of the select inner circle would have to move over and make room for Joe Hardy, who, after all, at twenty-one, still had his whole career ahead of him.

Joe grunted, letting the paper slip to the floor. He thought of all the grizzled veterans who had won their niches at Cooperstown only after hard labor over long years; and now he was being suggested as a fit companion for them. Ty Cobb, Babe Ruth—and Applegate. Applegate in the Hall of Fame. That's what it would amount to.

And suddenly he felt unclean, and even a little frightened.

The Boston series was notable for something else, and this concerned Applegate himself.

During the two games in New York, he and Lola had been in their accustomed seats along the right-field line. Joe had spoken to them briefly both nights, had learned that Applegate found the city very homelike. One morning he had gone to the top of the Statue of Liberty, and the following day he had spent riding the subways, covering the BMT system from one end to the other, even to all its tributaries. The rush hour, in particular, he had found absorbing. He seemed cheerful enough and gave no hint of anything abnormal.

But in Boston he turned up missing.

When Joe asked, Lola said all she knew was that Applegate had stayed on in New York to take care of some business.

On the face of it, this was no cause for concern. Applegate had his own life to live. Yet, in a very short time, he had become a fixture in Joe's life, the only continuing reality, and it was disconcerting to look out toward the right-field stands and find him missing.

And not only that . . . Abruptly Joe realized an even deeper implication of Applegate's absence, and felt fear crawl along his spine. If he should want Applegate, how would he get in touch with him? Suppose he never returned? Suppose he wasn't around on September twenty-first when the time came to be switched back?

It was a soul-clenching thought; a consideration the trusting Joe Boyd had never thought of. And, as always when he found reason to doubt Applegate's sincerity, he recalled the night the contract had been signed; recalled Applegate's undisguised, barely restrained glee.

The final stop on the eastern swing was Philadelphia, and although some may have found it a city of brotherly love, Joe left town with an entirely different impression.

Perusal of the daily box scores could not have told the full story, for in a baseball sense things went well. The team swept the series, stretching its victory skein to seventeen games.

But it was not of the box score that Joe was thinking when he went to bed on the night of the series opener. It was of the veteran Bobby Schantz who, that evening, had pitched perhaps the greatest game of an illustrious career, yet lost four to one.

It was a game long to be remembered by those who were witnesses. Schantz was superb. The Athletics shoved across a run in the first inning; thereafter they were impotent, but the way Schantz was pitching that run seemed ample. Entering the ninth, he still had his one-nothing lead, but more notable, he also had a no-hitter. Only three times had a Senator baserunner reached first, in each instance Joe Hardy. Working the corners a shade too minutely, Schantz had walked Joe in the first, again in the fourth, and again in the seventh.

In the ninth, while the fans sat tense and expectant, Schantz got the first two batters on pop-ups. It was then that his infield knifed him in the back. Two easy ground balls were bobbled; and Schantz, momentarily unsettled, walked the next batter. That brought up Joe Hardy again, with the bases loaded.

If ever a man faced a dilemma, that man was Bobby Schantz. To give Joe a deliberate base on balls meant forcing in a run, the loss of his shutout, and a tied ball game. Pitching to him, on the other hand, could mean not only the loss of his shutout but doom also to his hopes of a no-hitter. Only after a prolonged discussion with his catcher and with Manager Eddie Joost was a decision reached, and to the credit of Schantz it was the decision of a man who placed the team's welfare above his own.

For Joe could sense from the way Bobby walked back to the resin bag, from the way he turned resolutely toward the plate, that he had decided to gamble. A deliberate pass would mean conceding the Senators at least the tieing run that would keep them alive. Pitching to Joe, while the greater risk, at least meant that he was conceding nothing.

And standing there in the batter's box, gazing out toward the diminutive portsider, Joe felt a wave of pity. Here was Schantz, looking baseball immortality in the eye. Here was Joe Hardy with the power to deprive him of it. In all probability, Schantz, now in the late afternoon of a great career, would never come this close again to a no-hitter. It wouldn't hurt the Senators to lose this game. The Yanks had dropped a decision to the Red Sox that afternoon, so no ground could be lost. And Joe made a decision. He would offer only token swings. He would strike out.

On the first pitch he swung, weakly and purposely late, or so he thought . . .

And then watched with dismay as the ball went arching over the right-field wall. Stunned for a second, he did not move; then, with heavy heart, he began trotting around the bases, sadly noticing the slumped shoulders of Bobby Schantz; hearing the groans, tasting the melancholy of the Philadelphia fans.

This was worse than reading the column about the Hall of Fame.

What was it Applegate had said? "All you gotta do is swing. I'll do the rest."

And lying in bed that night, he felt he understood now how misery had come to Midas.

In actuality, Joe told himself, Bobby Schantz *had* pitched a no-hitter. In all *baseball* fact, he had won the ball game one to nothing. But it would never show that way in the record book.

The next morning, going down to breakfast, Joe had barely stepped from the elevator when his name rang across the lobby.

"Hey, Joe." It was Mr. van Buren, and he was brandishing a newspaper. "Did you see this?"

"What?"

"This guy Head. Look what he's writing."

A paragraph had been circled in pencil. It said:

"How good is too good? A week or so ago down in Washington, this column covered a press conference at which the young phenom Joe Hardy told reporters his home town was Hannibal, Missouri. It turns out that something is fishy and we don't mean the Mississippi. On the basis of careful investigation, this column now can say that nobody in the town of Hannibal, Missouri, ever heard of Joe Hardy before July 22. How about it, Joe? Why not come clean?"

Twice Joe read the paragraph and even after finishing he kept his head down, not ready yet to meet the eyes of Mr. van Buren.

"The guy's crazy," he said finally, with all the conviction he could muster. "What's he trying to do, anyway?"

"That's what I'd like to know," Mr. van Buren replied. "Of all the lousy sour grapes I've ever heard of . . . We gotta put him in his place, Joe. We gotta answer him. A couple of wire-service guys have called me already this morning."

Again Joe raised the paper and studied the paragraph. "Yeah, I guess we should," he said.

"For that matter you could sue him for libel if you want to," Mr. van Buren said.

"Yeah. I'm not sure he's worth it though."

"Well, we gotta give a statement to the press. That much

is certain," Mr. van Buren said. "What do you want me to tell 'em?"

"Let me write out something," Joe said. "Give me an hour or so while I have breakfast."

At breakfast he considered flight, considered waiting out the days until September twenty-first in some obscure corner of the world.

When he walked out to the lobby again, Mr. van Buren was not in sight, and Joe telephoned up to his room.

"Benny? Listen, I can't say it the way I want to. How about just ignoring the whole thing?"

"But listen, Joe, if we do that they'll think you're not on the level. Listen, you are from Hannibal, aren't you?"

"Of course I'm from Hannibal."

"Because if you're not, there's no sin in not being from Hannibal. But the point is we've gotta tell 'em something. Now suppose I just say that Joe Hardy completely denies Luster Head's charges, or something like that?"

For long seconds, Joe didn't answer. He was staring blankly at some brochures stacked next to the telephone. They advertised an air tour of the Caribbean.

"Is that all right with you?" Mr. van Buren asked.

"Yes, I guess so," Joe said. "Go ahead."

"Okay, maybe I'll use the word 'refutes' instead of 'denies.' It sounds better. All right, then. And listen, Joe . . . Don't let it get you down. Don't let it affect how you do out there this afternoon, hear?"

"Don't worry, Ben. Nothing like that can affect the way I play."

And he was right, to the tune of a home run and two doubles as the team notched a ten-to-two victory in the second game.

The next morning, with game time still several hours away, Joe was standing in a drug store just off the lobby of the hotel, watching with some others while Sammy Ransom played a pin-ball machine. Mr. van Buren had just finished a milkshake at the soda fountain and now sauntered over, his mind apparently at ease on the subject of Luster Head. Joe's denial had been given prominent space both in the evening and morning papers, and nothing further had been heard from Head.

During the team's long winning streak, Mr. van Buren had become a happy man. Yet, for apparently perverse reasons, Joe had noticed, this happiness manifested itself in a very sardonic sense of humor, of which no one had suspected him. Seeing the intent assemblage, he said, "If there's anything lower intellectually than playing a pin-ball machine, it's watching somebody else play one."

Joe looked up, smiled weakly, and then noticed a bell boy approaching with a telegram in hand. "For Mr. van Buren," he said.

Sensing disaster, Joe watched while Mr. van Buren tore at the envelope. But to judge from the latter's first reaction, Joe's fear was groundless. Mr. van Buren looked puzzled for a moment, then smiled faintly.

"Listen to this, boys. From Roscoe Ent. 'Hereby resign. Send final paycheck care of The Dirty Room, 13001 Winnipeg Street, Baltimore.'"

Mr. van Buren shook his head slowly. "Poor old Roscoe," he said. "He was his own worst enemy."

|11| A thunderstorm interrupted proceedings twice that afternoon, and it was seven o'clock before the game ended and close to eight before the team got on the train for Washington.

Joe sat alone in the rear of the car, staring out the window, not even joining the others in the diner. After the train pulled out, he drew a ham-and-cheese sandwich from the automatic vending machine and this was dinner. Ruminatively he munched it, looking out at the western sky, again somber with thunderheads, a sky already darkening when, on a clear night, there would have been another hour of summer twilight. It was a sky that matched his mood—although, he thought, watching the swiftly scudding clouds in the southwest, it was also a sky that had more guts than he had. Joe Hardy, born Boyd, although lithe and limber in body, was becoming a spineless pawn.

It was getting to be lousy, all of it. Compounding the lie about Hannibal made it lousy. Robbing Schantz of his no-hitter made it lousy, but most of all Roscoe Ent made it lousy. For if, according to all normal standards, Schantz had really pitched his no-hitter, shouldn't Ent by the same standards still have his job, pathetic though it may have been?

Absently balling the waxed paper from his sandwich, he thought again of Applegate's cocky smile and pondered whether Applegate himself might not be deliberately responsible for the unfortunate turn of events. Or were they simply inherent, inevitable, in the role Joe was playing? But on the other hand, the role he was playing was Applegate's doing too, and it was hard to separate one line of reasoning from the other.

Even after the team came back from the diner, Joe continued to sit somberly alone. Around him were sounds of jubilation. There was talk of the pennant. The Red Sox had edged the Yankees again that afternoon. Another game picked up. But looking about at the happy faces, Joe could not share their jubilation.

Looking out the window again, he was reminded for no apparent reason of a night during the Quebec trip when he and Bess had been caught near dark with no place to spend the night, and had driven until almost midnight before they found one. He felt a stab of nostalgia. That night seemed long ago.

There was Mr. Welch and there was Mr. van Buren. There were the fans, miserable as he had been for so many years, and now given hope. There was the thrill in running from the dugout at game time, taking the field with the team; standing out in right field with his cap off while the National Anthem was played; the thrill of feeling bat meet ball and knowing it had been well met. There were the years of frustration and of yearning; the box scores of a thousand and one nights, and more: the pain of these to efface.

Yet, in spite of all these things, he knew at that moment that if he had the power he would quit being Joe Hardy, there and then.

But it would be weeks yet before he had the power, and involuntarily he twisted in his seat. It was as though he could actually feel the strait jacket.

For the most part the team respected Joe's solitude, although Mr. van Buren had shown troubled eyes going to the diner and again coming back from it, and finally, just below Aberdeen, dropped into the seat beside him.

"What's the trouble, Joe? Something got you down?"

Joe stopped shredding the waxed paper and let it drop to the floor. "No," he said. "Just tired, I guess."

"You're not worried about Luster Head, are you?"

"No, I'm not worried about him."

"I don't think we'll hear any more out of that guy," Mr. van Buren said. "He shut up quick. Listen, it's not Ent that's bothering you, is it?"

Joe hesitated. "Well, some, I guess."

"Aw, Joe, that's silly. You're not to blame."

"Well, technically I guess I am. If it hadn't been for me, he'd still have his job."

"That's no way to look at it, Joe. Besides, he could still have his job if he wanted it. We didn't fire the guy. He quit. He just acted like a spoiled brat, that's all. And furthermore he never belonged in baseball in the first place. It was kind of an insult to have him around. Did you ever hear about his background?"

Joe shook his head.

"Well, let me tell you about him." Mr. van Buren drew a cigar from his vest, settled back and began the story of Roscoe Ent's life, while Joe listened moodily.

A man doomed by nature to the shortest of stature, Roscoe Ent had been born near Pocomoke, Maryland, where his people owned a sausage factory. At an early age, probably right after high school, Mr. van Buren thought, Roscoe had forsworn the sausage factory and left home for Baltimore, where he landed a job as shipping clerk and where he also developed a strong attachment for the local burlesque house. When not on the job, he could almost invariably be found at the theater. Whether because he felt an attachment for the dancing and stripping girls or because he loved the genially rowdy atmosphere, Mr. van Buren was unable to say for certain. In any event, he had become such an habitué that he soon was able to ingratiate himself with the management, and in a very short time he had talked himself into a job as prop man, leaving the shipping business behind for good and all.

For one so dedicated as Roscoe, it apparently had been but a short step from the prop to the performing end of the business, and it was not long before he had bit parts in the comedy sketches, first as straight man and later as a comedian in his own right.

As time went on, Mr. van Buren said, Roscoe became a very important drawing card, often getting co-billing with the featured stripper. Dressed always in checkered and very baggy trousers and a necktie that reached to the floor, he featured a peculiarly unique method of dancing, a kind of one-legged shuffle with the other leg bent beneath him. He was also considered a master of pained, sorrowful facial expressions.

Firmly established in this sinecure, Roscoe was offered many chances to go around the wheel, to go, that is, from city to city with the traveling burlesque troupes. But he loved Baltimore and Baltimore loved him, and in Baltimore he remained, a fixture, more than happy, far from the sausage factory, far from death.

Happy, that is, until the demise of burlesque. The danger signs had appeared in the 1940's. By 1950 at least half the houses on the wheel were closed, but a few strongholds, Baltimore among them, held out staunchly. But even these doughty bastions, beset by night clubs and TV, were forced to give it up eventually, and it was in 1955 that Roscoe found himself, one day, standing dolefully before the closed doors of the ornate old building, out of a job.

By this time, Roscoe Ent was thirty-five.

It struck him then that his talents might be of value to the Washington Senators. The Baltimore Orioles were near at hand, but they were riding high. With the Senators, falling attendance was a grave problem.

"And so we hired him," Mr. van Buren continued. "It pained me to do it, but after all, the old St. Louis Browns once sent a midget up to bat. We weren't the first. Roscoe really wasn't a bad guy. And actually, he discovered he could throw a dinkey little curve. It just griped me to have him around on general principles. I felt more like a ringmaster than a manager. . . . Listen, Joe, why don't you go on up to the diner and get something to eat. You've still got some time."

"I'm not hungry," Joe said. "I had a sandwich."

Mr. van Buren looked at him skeptically. Then, gesticulating with the cigar, he said, "Look, Joe. When you stop to think about it, here's what Ent is saying. He's saying if you guys aren't going to be a lousy ball club any more, then I won't play. Now what the hell kind of an attitude is that?"

"I guess you're right," Joe said.

"Sure I'm right, boy. Stop worrying about Roscoe Ent. Well, we picked up another game on the Yankees today."

"Yeah, I know. That's fine."

Mr. van Buren left him then, to take part in a discussion of batting strokes up the aisle.

Joe slumped low in his seat. What Mr. van Buren had been saying in effect, he realized, was that Roscoe Ent's life was unimportant, even ridiculous. But it was no less important than other lives. It was too late now to do anything about Schantz's no-hitter. But there was still time to do the decent thing where Ent was concerned. And never had there been a time in his life when Joe must be so particular to do the decent thing. Each time he failed, Applegate would gain.

At Baltimore, he slipped unnoticed from the train.

12	Except for frontage and its name, The Dirty Room would have been indistinguishable from any of a score or more night clubs in its immediate neon-suffused area. Of front-

age, it could boast no more than the width of a railroad car, wedged as it was between a pair of establishments known as The Silver Thread and Herbert's.

A railroad car, in fact, rather closely described it, Joe thought, walking in and taking a seat at the small bar just inside the door. It was in truth a corridor of a place, crowded with patrons who sat at tables no greater in diameter than a kitchen stool and barely large enough to accommodate a couple of glasses and an ash tray.

All patrons' eyes at the moment were on a small stage at the far end where a girl was dancing, dressed ostensibly only in a one-piece togalike garment of lavender gauze. As Joe ordered a beer and turned to watch, the girl whistled; obediently, from somewhere in the room, a macaw flew up to the stage, speaking the words, "Here I am now." Grasping the garment in its beak, the macaw deftly tugged; the garment fell away, and the girl was revealed with very little on. There was hearty applause as she made a bounc- ing exit, the macaw perched now on her wrist and still squawking, "Here I am now."

She was replaced by a florid individual, carrying a glass of beer, who hurried out to the microphone and spoke as follows:

"Yes, sir, ladies and gentlemen, a big hand for our little Sandra, everybody's sweetheart, and her macaw."

The speaker set his beer down to clap chubby hands in the direction of the wing, and then resumed:

"And now ladies and gentlemen, the event you've been waiting for. The Dirty Room is now honored to bring you back a name that needs no introduction to Baltimore; once a popular favorite with burlesque fans of every description, and more recently a great favorite at the Washington baseball organization; ladies and gentlemen, we bring you fresh from his triumphs in baseball, making his maiden return appearance in this city, our good friend and yours, who will act as our master of ceremonies throughout the remainder of each and every act; our good friend without further ado, that funny little fellow, *Ros*-coe ENT!"

And Roscoe, dressed as Joe had never seen him, shuffled out with a complex of leg movements difficult to follow, although reminiscent of the movement of a pair of scissors. Wearing a checkered suit with baggy trousers, a black derby, and a bow tie of vast wing span, he stood for a moment at the microphone, looking deadpan about the room. There was anticipatory laughter.

Still deadpan, he began:

"I was coming over here tonight and a guy comes up to me and he says, 'Hey, buddy, haven't I seen you some place before?' And I says to him, 'I don't know, have you?' And he says, 'Yeah, wasn't you out with my sister last night?' And I says, 'I didn't know you had a sister,' and he says, 'I haven't.' Then he nodded and walked off. I'd never seen the guy in my life."

"Yes sir," Roscoe said, strutting about the microphone and rubbing his hands. "Yes, sir."

But from the audience there was only light laughter.

"Don't like that one?" Roscoe asked. "All right, how about another one? There was this guy and his wife gave a party, see? Down in their recreation room. And the guy proceeds to get very loaded, and all during the party he pays plenty of attention to a girl there, let's call her Mae. So about seven o'clock next morning, after the party's over for hours and everybody supposed to be gone, this guy's wife wakes up and notices he's missing from the bed. She hears a noise down in the recreation room, so she gets out of bed and goes to the head of the stairs and yells, 'Who's down there?' And her husband yells back, 'It's me and Mae. Who's that?'"

"Yes, sir," Roscoe said, rubbing his hands again, "Who's that?" And this time a bulb glowed at the center of his bow tie.

But from the audience there was no laughter, and furthermore a few groans.

Roscoe looked at them narrowly and then, turning to the wing, called, "There's some people out here just died. Get a hearse."

Hands on hips, he said, "I'll try one more on you charming people. . . . This guy took a girl out in his car, see? And all during the ride she kept shaking her head 'no.' It was thirty-five miles before he realized she had her nose caught in the windshield wiper."

Although there were no groans, the laughter was still thin and, watching intently, Joe saw the bravado fade from Ent's face, replaced for an instant by despair.

"'At guy stinks," the bartender said. "I thought he was supposed to be funny, or something."

For a few seconds, Roscoe seemed about to retreat to the wings, but instead he doffed his derby, flipped it into the air, and caught it squarely on his head as it came down.

Somebody in the audience booed.

Roscoe stiffened, and he walked slowly around before the microphone. "What's the matter with you people out there? Where do you think you are, anyway? At a wake?"

"I've been to funnier wakes," somebody shouted.

"Maybe you'd rather go up the street," Roscoe said derisively. "I understand up the street they have a very funny act—a couple guys wrestling on top of a great big pile of dead fish. Very funny."

Suddenly, at a signal unseen to Joe, the three-piece band began playing with as much volume as possible.

"Sounds pretty funny to me," the same patron shouted.

"Yeah, but is it funny for the fish?" Roscoe demanded over the sound of the band.

"The fish is all dead."

"Well, why don't you go up there and see it then?" Roscoe screamed.

· 107 ·

"Bring on Sandra and the bird again," somebody yelled.

At this point the same florid man who had introduced him hurried into the stage and, hooking an arm through Roscoe's, ushered him toward the wing, managing to clap at the same time.

A lean man in a double-breasted suit was rushed to the stage and began playing a harmonica with the mien of a man bailing out a boat.

A few of the patrons, and then a few more, got up to leave. The harmonica player went at it more feverishly, with bobbing of head and furrowing of brow.

In a moment the florid man was back, raising his hands for quiet. "Ladies and gentlemen," he said then, "as a special added attraction, our own little Sandra and her macaw, who always usually only does the one number per floor show, has kindly consented to do us another number. In a few seconds, it will be Sandra. And now—on with BOB and his harMONICA."

The patrons slowly settled back into their seats.

The dressing-room door was open a crack and Joe paused at the threshold. He could see Roscoe sitting at a makeshift dressing table, contrived from an orange crate and covered with newspaper. His derby lay on the floor.

"I don't get it, Ros, I just don't get it." The speaker was out of sight, although Joe judged it was the florid man who had introduced Roscoe, evidently the owner. "Boy, you ain't like you used to be when you was over the Lyceum. Don't seem to me like you got your heart into it."

"It's the audience that's changed, not me," Roscoe said in a tone that lacked conviction. "Can I help it if your customers ain't got no sense of humor?"

"Suppose they ain't? Is that any reason to go getting nasty about the fish and all? Whaddya trying to do, lose me all the business I got? It's an old proverb—nobody never won any argument with no customers yet."

"Okay, so I'm sorry," Roscoe said, yanking off his bow tie and flinging it. "So I won't be around to bother you any more."

"Look, Ros, I'm sorry. I tried to help you out, but I can't take a chance. It's tough enough to make a living as it is."

"Okay, so I'll go."

"Where you gonna go?"

Roscoe sighed. "I don't know yet."

"To work for your old man in the factory?"

"Maybe."

For a while there was the sound of heavy pacing, and then: "Look, Ros, how about giving another try tomorrow night? It's okay with me. Maybe you get some new lines and stuff . . ."

"No," Roscoe said. "I think you're right. My heart ain't in it no more, Max. I don't know what it is. Maybe I'm spoiled from baseball." Again he sighed. "Sometimes you feel like being funny and sometimes you don't."

"That was the biggest mistake you ever made, going over to that baseball," Max said, and with these words he opened the door and brushed past Joe without even a show of curiosity. Stalking down the plywood-partitioned corridor, he stopped at the only other door and called, "Hey, baby, ain't you ready yet? That slob can't play the mouth organ all night."

"This damn bird stole all my bobby pins," a woman's voice replied.

As Joe stepped into the room, Ent was slumped over the orange crate. "Roscoe," Joe said.

Ent turned and regarded him without surprise. "Well, if it ain't Joe flashy-pants," he said. "I saw you back there at the bar. I might as well known my goose was cooked with you here, you lousy jinxer, you. How'd you know where I was?"

"The telegram you sent van Buren. We were coming down from Philadelphia and I got off here. Listen, Roscoe, I'd like to talk to you a minute."

"We ain't got nothing to talk about, Hardy," Roscoe said. Picking up his derby, he held it under one arm, an inexplicably protective gesture.

"Come on out and have a beer with me," Joe said. "I want to talk to you about the team."

At that moment his eye fell on the newspaper covering the orange crate. Staring up at him was a picture of Luster Head, and it was the column with the crack about Joe and Hannibal. Roscoe, even as Mr. van Buren, had circled the paragraph with a pencil.

Ent followed Joe's glance and, leering slightly, said, "What is it you want to tell me, Hardy?" Chuckling, he rose, and Joe could not help noting that Roscoe was far less imposing standing than seated. "You gonna tell me you're a phony? A ringer? I already guessed that long ago."

"Listen, Roscoe . . ." Joe began.

But Roscoe was already listening, head cocked and frowning. From outside there now came loud laughter, spontaneous and uncontrolled, the laughter of an audience held captive.

"Who's so funny?" Roscoe muttered.

Putting on his derby, he hurried out, Joe following. Max, with a pleased expression, and the harmonica player stood in the wing. "Who's so funny?" Roscoe repeated.

"It was just some guy in the audience," the harmonica player said. "Guy just walked up to the stage and said he'd like to do a number." He broke off, laughing heartily.

Joe stood at a distance. "How about that beer, Roscoe?" he said.

"Wait a minute," Roscoe said, craning his neck around the harmonica player's elbow. "Okay," he said, "I'll watch him from outside. Come on, Hardy. I'll promise to drink a glass of beer if you promise to drink a glass of rat poison. Okay?"

"I wish you wouldn't feel that way, Roscoe."

"Okay, old pal," Roscoe said, reaching up and clapping Joe on the back. "I got nothing but esteem for you, old pal, because you made me lose my job, old pal." Looking up at Joe, he scowled.

They took a table at the rear, and when Joe looked toward the stage and recognized the performer he didn't even feel surprise. Not that he had any reason to suspect; it was simply that anything connected with Applegate was no longer surprising.

For the performer was Applegate. Applegate dressed in his gray suit and snap-brim, and saying now, "Who was that ladle I seen you out with last night? That was no ladle, that was my knife."

Roscoe groaned and held his nose, but his reaction was lost in the rising swell of laughter.

It was then that Applegate spied Joe and, waving, he called, "Hi, Joe, how's the boy? Long time, no see. Ladies and gentlemen, in case you don't know it, you've got a celebrity in your midst tonight. That fresh-faced lad back there with the crew cut, sitting with the little fellow in the derby hat, is none other than the fabulous Joe Hardy of the Washington baseball club."

Not half the celebrity you are, Joe thought sardonically, but he stood and bowed. Heads turned and cheers went up.

"Yes, sir," Applegate said, striking his hat against his leg. "You never know what kind of celebrities you're gonna run into at the Dirty Room. Right, Max?"

Max, beaming, stepped from the wing, waved, and stepped back again.

As Applegate launched again into his routine, Ent said bitterly, "I've seen some crumby guys in my life, Hardy, but you're about the crumbiest. What is this, a put-up job between you and your friend up there to kill my act?"

Joe shook his head, smiling sadly. "Everywhere I turn

I seem to put my foot in it as far as you're concerned, Roscoe. . . . I didn't know he was going to be here to-night."

"Well, what did you have to come for yourself?"

"Mostly to apologize," Joe said, "and to see if I could per-suade you to go back to the team. I don't see why you had to quit in the first place."

"Listen, Hardy, I may not be the big shot you are, but even little shots got some pride. Think I was gonna suck around a job like that anymore? I could tell nobody wanted me. All anybody thought about any more was winning ball games."

"You can't blame a team for that," Joe said.

"Those Washington Senators got no business even think-ing about winning," Roscoe said. "I had that figured for a lifetime job."

"It can still be a lifetime job," Joe said.

"I'm tellin' ya, I don't go where I'm not wanted," Roscoe said. "I'm not wanted on the team, I quit. I'm not wanted here tonight, I quit. I ain't gonna be no burden."

"Do you have any family, Roscoe?"

"I got my parents is all. What's that got to do with it?" He shook his head in disgust. "That guy stinks out loud."

Joe turned. Applegate now wore a straw hat. Grasping a walking stick loosely before him, he was engaged in a soft-shoe maneuver, while singing, "When the red red robin comes bob-bob-bobbin' along."

"And besides that, he's homely," Roscoe said. He turned

to Joe again and a sly expression came into his rather pro-truding dark eyes. "Okay, Hardy, so what's that thing you were gonna tell me in the dressing room?"

"Will you take my word for something, Roscoe?"

"Why should I?"

"Because it's to your own advantage. Here's what I've got to tell you. Go back and keep your job and I'll give you my word that in a few weeks everything will be back to normal again. The team'll be glad to have you there for next season."

"How come?"

"That's all I can tell you," Joe said. "You'll just have to take my word for it. And don't tell anybody I told you, either."

"Okay, so where's your home town?" Roscoe said, pleased with himself.

"That doesn't concern you or anybody else," Joe said. "All I'm trying to do is help you."

"It's not Sing Sing by any chance, is it?" Roscoe asked, leering.

"Cut it out, Roscoe. I'm trying to help you."

There was a thunderous burst of applause, to which Applegate responded with repeated bows, then jumped nimbly from the stage and threaded his way among the tables.

"Joseph, Joseph," he said fondly, pulling up a chair. "Draw me a milk, madam," he said to the waitress. "With a little cheese. Joseph, my boy, how's it going? I see you're in good company tonight."

"Mr. Applegate, Mr. Ent," Joe said grimly.

"Sure, I've seen Mr. Ent at the games," Applegate said jovially. They shook hands. "How are you, Ent?"

"Seems to me I've seen you before too," Ent said.

"Sure, I've been to a lot of games lately," Applegate said, putting his hat on a chair, and beginning to finger his forelock.

"I don't mean at no games, I mean a long time ago," Roscoe said. "Did you ever hang around burlesque by any chance?"

"I've seen a burlesque show or two in my time, I daresay," Applegate replied. "I can't honestly say I've hung around it though."

"Did you ever know a tall, loose-jointed guy named Hathawell? A comedian?"

"Hathawell? No, I can't say that I ever knew any Hathawells."

Ent looked dubious. "There's a guy he used to go out for a drink with all the time, looked exactly like you," he persisted. "He was about the luckiest guy I ever knew in my life, that guy Hathawell. Inherited a million bucks from some uncle he never even knew he had. After that he dropped out of burlesque."

"His friend must have been my double," Applegate said, laughing heartily. Spreading his hands on the table, he said, "Well, Joseph, and how's it going with you, my boy? I see by the papers you had a splendid road trip."

Joe looked at him darkly. "What else did you see in the papers?"

"What else? Oh. Oh-h-h. That was a snide thing that Mr. Head wrote, wasn't it now?"

Ent was looking from one to the other with great curiosity.

Applegate's right hand still lay flat on the table, and Joe saw the index finger move slightly and point to Ent who, although he did not notice, nevertheless rose immediately, as if in alarm. "Excuse me, I've got to go to the little boys' room," he said, hurrying off.

"Rather clever, eh?" Applegate said when he had gone.

"Listen, Applegate," Joe said, "I don't mind telling you I don't like the way things are going."

"Oh, come now, Joe." Applegate smiled, looking toward the stage. "The little girl is quite a dish now, isn't she? I wonder if she's pleased with her lot."

Sandra had just been introduced for her second number.

"It's a wonder you don't have Lola up there," Joe said.

"No," Applegate said. "Strip work is not Lola's line. Lola is too refined for that sort of thing. . . ." His voice faded as he sat looking speculatively toward the stage.

"Maybe you'd like to sign up the macaw too," Joe said sarcastically.

"No, the macaw would make it inconvenient," Applegate said, still facing the stage. He turned back to Joe. "In fact, I don't think I particularly go for Sandra either. Now Joe, what's on your mind, lad? I'm sorry I haven't been around. I've been pretty busy lately."

"I told you I don't like the way things are going."

"For instance?"

"For instance, Roscoe Ent."

"What about him?"

"He's lost his job and it's my fault."

Applegate arched his heavy brows. "You mean you feel soft-hearted about Ent?"

"I feel sorry for him."

"Well . . ." Applegate wet his forefinger and went about the table, gathering crumbs of cheese. "Come to think of it, the little fellow has had a tough go of it lately, for a fact. Now maybe we could make redress to him."

Joe looked up suspiciously. "What kind of redress?" he asked.

"I don't know," Applegate said innocently. "Something appropriate."

"Yeah, with what kind of strings attached?"

"Strings?"

"It wouldn't hurt you to do something once in a while out of the kindness of your heart," Joe said. "Without strings."

"Now, Joe, I do plenty of things out of the kindness of my heart. Who bought you those clothes you're wearing?" Applegate looked off toward the opposite wall with a bemused expression. "But Mr. Ent certainly has had an incredible streak of bad luck, for certain."

"Lay off," Joe said.

Applegate looked hurt. "Joe . . ." he said. "Don't be unpleasant. We're having a nice evening out together . . ."

"I said lay off him," Joe said.

"Joe, honestly, you're hurting me right in here . . ." Applegate tapped the region of his heart.

"All I want Ent to do is go take his old job back," Joe said. "So let's leave it at that. And now I want to talk to you about me. What's—"

He broke off, because at that moment three young ladies appeared at his elbow and one, offering half a menu, said, "Could I please have your autograph, Mr. Hardy?"

"You're a very discriminating autograph seeker, my dear," Applegate said. "He's the greatest ball player of the century."

"You ought to get *his* autograph," Joe said. "Then you'd really have something."

"Oh, Joe," Applegate said deprecatingly.

Joe signed his name, then signed again and again, and when he looked up, he saw the line had grown. He also saw that Applegate had disappeared. Once more he signed, then looked about the room. Neither Applegate nor Ent was in sight. Jumping up, he hurried back to the men's room. No sign of Ent. No sign of Applegate.

13 Joe had circled the block and started off at a new tangent, when, far ahead, he thought he spied them. A tall figure and a much shorter figure, a block away. The hand of the taller was on the shoulder of the smaller. Joe began to run.

As he drew near, Applegate, without turning, called "Hi, Joe. Mr. Ent and I were just going to have a little talk. I'm glad you joined us."

"Hardy joins everybody everyplace they go," Ent said.

"Yes, Joe is a very gregarious sort," Applegate said, clapping Ent's shoulder. "Did you get all your autographs signed, Joe?"

"Listen," Joe said, pulling abreast, "What are you up to, Applegate?"

"I told you Mr. Ent and I are going to have a little talk. And why not?"

"Why don't you blow, Hardy?" Ent said. They were walking now through what apparently was a business district, between walls of darkened buildings. "Why don't you go catch a pop fly, or something?" Ent chuckled and Applegate laughed appreciatively. "Roscoe," he said, "you've really got quite a sense of humor, boy."

"Listen, Applegate," Joe said ominously.

"This, uh—well, I don't really know what part of speech it is," Applegate said, "but you're always saying 'listen.' Listen this and listen that. It gets tiresome."

"Now listen here, Applegate . . ."

"See what I mean? It gets tiresome, doesn't it, Mr. Ent?"

"Very tiresome," Ent agreed.

"I told you to lay off," Joe said.

"Oh, come now, Joe. Let us alone, lad. Go finish signing your autographs."

Ent stopped before a gray structure which now lacked even a marquee. The building and those around it were dark. "This is where the theater used to be," he said in the tone of one resuming a broken conversation.

"Well, this seems a rather fitting spot, then, doesn't it?" Applegate said.

"Applegate, I'm warning you," Joe said.

"Listen, Joe," Applegate said with irritation, "You live your life and I'll live mine. Fair enough?"

"You're really beginning to show your true colors now, aren't you?" Joe asked grimly.

"Just trying to help out a fellow who's had a bad run of luck," Applegate said. "You said yourself you felt sorry for him, but you weren't doing anything about it. Me, I'm doing something about it."

"Blow, Hardy," Ent said.

"Well," Applegate said, "as long as he won't blow, I suppose we'll have to proceed anyway. Now Mr. Ent," he went on, clapping Roscoe on the shoulder, "of all the courses available to you, which would you prefer? To join your father in his sausage factory? To be a very successful song-and-dance and funny man? To have your old job back with the team? Or, and this may surprise you, to be a bona fide major-league pitcher?"

"Pitcher?" Roscoe echoed. "How'm I gonna be any pitcher?"

With guilt in his heart, Joe remembered the similar question he had asked the night Applegate had first appeared.

"Just take my word for it," Applegate said. "You can be a pitcher, a fabulously successful pitcher, replete with sliders and sinkers and hooks and pinpoint control and blinding speed—such a pitcher as has not been seen since the days of Christy Mathewson and Walter Johnson."

Roscoe laughed. "I think you're pulling my leg," he said.

"Not in the slightest, Roscoe," Applegate said. "Do you mind if I call you Roscoe? And you can call me App, if you like. That's what my friends call me."

Again Roscoe chuckled dubiously. Joe paced out to the curb, looked up and down the dark street, and returned, standing helplessly.

"Look, Roscoe," Applegate was saying. "Suppose you take your pitcher's stance. That's right. Now go into your motion and follow through. . . . I know you've done some pitching before, but doesn't it feel different somehow?"

"It sure does," Roscoe said, straightening up again. "Co-ordination seems better somehow."

"That's it, co-ordination," Applegate said.

"I feel like I could throw a ball through the side of a locomotive somehow," Roscoe said.

"Right, Roscoe. Cigarette?"

"No, thanks."

And Joe saw Applegate light his own with the now familiar snap of his fingers. This was not lost on Roscoe, who said admiringly, "Hey! That would kill 'em back in The Dirty Room. How about teaching me?"

"That's not something you teach somebody," Joe said.

Applegate chuckled. "Not so much noise, Hardy. So, Roscoe, my boy, how would you like to be a pitcher?"

"What's the deal?" Roscoe said.

"What's the deal?" Applegate clapped him on the shoulder. "Here's a forthright man, Hardy. No hemming and hawing and beating about the bush. Well, Roscoe, exactly what the deal is we can discuss later. The main thing I'd like to know first is whether you'd like to be a pitcher?"

"Say no, Roscoe," Joe said quickly. "Tell him no."

"Hardy, do you have to butt into everything I do?" Ent demanded. "First thing I know you'll be—"

"I'm telling you this for your own good, Roscoe," Joe said. "Tell him no."

Applegate stood by, chuckling quietly, with the attitude of a man who had nothing at stake. Or, Joe thought with a disquieting feeling, a man who wins no matter what the outcome.

"So why should I tell him no?" Roscoe said.

"Roscoe," Joe asked, glancing swiftly at Applegate, "don't you know who this man is?"

"What do you mean, who he is?"

"Did you see how he lit that cigarette?"

"I've seen guys do that in burlesque," Roscoe said. "Come on now, Hardy, let us alone. Go sign your autographs."

"Roscoe, doesn't that brain of yours work at all?"

"Don't insult me, Hardy."

"Roscoe . . ." There was a low, distant rumble of thunder in the east. ". . . this guy isn't any song and dance man. He's the devil."

For a few seconds no one spoke. A taxi sped past. From another direction came a squad car, which slowed as it neared the theater entrance. Applegate impatiently snapped his fingers, and it passed on.

"The devil!" Roscoe said hoarsely. He edged away from Applegate. "Is Hardy serious?"

Applegate drew himself up to his full height. "I've never been one to deny my roots," he said pompously.

"I don't believe it," Roscoe said. "I don't—"

But without finishing, he turned and ran with the speed of a sprinter. Joe watched as the small form faded into the darkness. Even afterward he could hear the tap of his feet on the sidewalk. Finally he could hear no more.

Joe turned, fearful of Applegate for the first time since they had met. But Applegate was chuckling. "The one that got away," he said. "That was quite a spectacle," he went on admiringly. "The little fellow really can run, can't he, Joe?"

"Is that all you've got to say?"

Again Applegate chuckled. "Joe, somehow you amuse me tonight beyond all reason. I suppose you feel very proud of yourself."

"I wasn't going to let you get away with it," Joe said.

"For instance, the way you speak of 'letting' me do things is tremendously amusing, Joe. Ah, Joe, what an attitude. I was only trying to help out a guy who'd been having a run of bad luck. I never dreamed you'd take such a disapproving attitude. You've changed since I last saw you."

"I've changed plenty," Joe said. "I'm sick of this whole lousy business. I want you to change me back. Right now. Tonight."

"You're a little bit premature, lad. This isn't September twenty-first in the slightest. Remember the contract."

"Nuts to the contract," Joe said. "Somebody who just tried to pull something like that wouldn't pay any attention to a contract anyway. Come on now, you lousy four-flusher . . ."

Again Applegate chuckled, but stopped abruptly. "Joe, don't tax my sense of humor too far, lad. I like a certain amount of spunk, but when it becomes downright rude-ness . . . well, just remember one thing, Joe. I'm still the only one can turn Joe Hardy back into Joe Boyd . . . and remember I've been pretty good to you, all things considered. So maybe you'd better be a little more respect-ful . . ."

Joe stared Applegate defiantly in the eye. "You mean you refuse?"

"Yes, I must refuse, lad, but . . ."

Joe blinked to clear the film from his eyes, but there was no film. Applegate had simply disappeared, in mid-sentence. From no direction that he could tell, there came another clap of thunder and then, out of the thunder, Applegate's voice, seeming to rise high above the city.

". . . but I can assure you this, Joe. I'll respect the contract to the letter. Right down to the last letter."

It was said in an oily voice, a mocking voice, heavy with irony, and Joe shivered. Feeling frightened and suddenly very small, he searched the sky, listened attentively. But Applegate spoke no more.

14 Although the schedule called for an off-day, Mr. van Buren, flushed with pennant fever, had the team out for batting practice all next afternoon, making ready for the long home stand coming up against the western clubs, initially the Cleveland Indians.

He was inquiring about Joe's health when Joe spied Lola taking a seat in her customary box; Lola, looking tanned and lissome, cool and poised, in a sleeveless white summer dress with a green sash.

"You look a little pale around the gills to me," Mr. van Buren said, grunting as he fungoed another fly out to left field. "And incidentally, Joe, I missed you after the train pulled out of Baltimore last night. What happened?"

"I got off there," Joe said, his eyes still on Lola. "There's an old friend of mine I hadn't seen for a long time. I promised him I'd drop by."

"That's not the old friend sitting over there by herself in the right-field stands, is it?" Mr. van Buren asked slyly. He dropped the bat and turned to look at Lola.

"No, that's another friend," Joe said.

"Not that I'd blame you," Mr. van Buren said admiringly. "She must be quite a fan if she even comes out to watch batting practice. I wonder what the attraction is," he said, rubbing his hands on his pants and picking up the bat again.

"I'm not sure myself," Joe said. "Excuse me a second, will you, Ben?"

He noticed how grave were Lola's lavender eyes, how immobile her exquisite face as she watched him approach.

"Tonight?" she said when he had asked. "Well, it seems to me that the last time we were alone together you left me stranded in a traffic jam. I'm not sure where I'd be immune from desertion. Unless maybe in a canoe." She smiled, lowering her eyes.

"I'm sorry about leaving you that day," Joe said. "But, Lola, this is pretty important. I need your help."

"On the other hand," she went on archly, "even if we took a canoe, you might swim to shore, and it would be tiresome to be stranded in a moving canoe. But I guess a canoe is as safe as any."

"Are you serious about the canoe?" he asked. "Okay, anywhere you say, only I've never paddled a canoe in my life."

"Oh, that doesn't matter," she said. "You should know that doesn't matter, Joe."

Silently Joe dipped the blade, impressed in spite of himself by the deftness and power of his stroke. In darkness the canoe shot forward in an unveering line, approaching now the Key Bridge, and when they moved beneath it Lola, in the bow, whistled softly. A small echo answered from the concrete pilings, went rolling up around the arch above their heads. It was now a little after ten, and they had just cleared the boathouse.

"See," Lola said, trailing her hand in the water. "You paddle beautifully, Joe. You could probably win a paddling championship, if you wanted to."

They passed on from the bridge, gliding swiftly downstream.

"Winning a paddling championship isn't what's on my mind right now," Joe said. "It's your friend Applegate."

"I thought that's probably why you wanted to see me," she said somberly.

"Lola, I need your help," Joe said. "Or at least I think I do. Except—"

"Except what, Joe?"

He shipped the paddle, letting the canoe float, noticing the graceful line her shoulders made in the white cardigan. Downstream, beyond her head, car lights moved along the drive. From somewhere across the river, from an invisible canoe perhaps, laughter floated over the water and died.

"Well," he said, "I don't know how I stand with you. I suppose it's not too important, but—on the other hand I think it is important. Will you answer me one question truthfully? Are you hooked?"

"Hooked?"

"You know what I mean."

She did not reply at once, intently smoothing the surface of the water with her palm. Finally, she said, "Yes, Joe, I am."

Joe sighed. "Well, we've got that much settled anyway."

"Although," she went on, "I'm not sure hooked is the right word to use. But . . . maybe it is."

"Gosh, Lola," he said "Why did you do it?"

She laughed softly. "Why did I do it? Oh, a lot of reasons, most of them very personal. Don't worry about me, Joe."

"Are you on a permanent basis?"

"Yes, quite permanent."

He dipped the blade, pulling it back with one long stroke, and again shipped it.

"Poor Lola," he said.

"I'm not really an object of pity, Joe. It happened quite a while ago, and I'm quite used to it in many ways. . . . What did you want to ask me about Mr. Applegate?"

For a while he did not reply, and they moved in silence, broken only by the swirling sound of the water as he dipped the blade; then by a plane which roared up from the take-off and passed overhead.

Presently he said, "Let me ask you this, Lola. Were you ever on a temporary basis? A trial period? You know what I mean."

"Yes. I can even recall the big day. It was May four-teenth."

He stopped paddling, fearing her answer to his next question. "Did you plan for it to be permanent?" he asked.

"No," she said. "I thought I'd just have a taste of it, but when May fourteenth came Mr. Applegate was far too smart for me, it turned out. He's very farsighted."

From an island off to the right, a night bird screeched and the sound became thin and then faded as the bird flew rapidly off.

With a chill running along his spine, Joe asked, "What happened? How was he too smart for you?"

"I'm afraid I can't tell you that, Joe."

"Why not?"

"I just can't," she said. "I'd like to but I can't."

"Well, what did he do? Did he break the contract?"

"Oh, no," she said. "Mr. Applegate always lives up to his contracts. He really does."

"Well then, what did he do?"

"It was very subtle," she said in a tone of reminiscence.

"Well he's not going to fool me!" Joe burst out, but he realized there was more bravado in his voice than conviction. "Do you hear?" he demanded when she made no reply.

"Yes, I hear, Joe."

"How *could* he? He can't."

"I hope you're right," Lola said quietly.

Cursing under his breath, he paddled swiftly. The river bent to the right, bringing the lights of Memorial Bridge into view.

"Joe . . . Don't fight it. There's no use."

With a laugh meant to be sarcastic, he said, "Huh! That's what you think, baby."

"Not with me, Joe. Don't be angry with me."

"Well then, what makes you say he's got me?"

"I hope I'm wrong, but I know I'm right," she said.

"Huh! We'll see when September twenty-first comes."

"Well, if it comes—and goes—at least you'll have the satisfaction of knowing that your cause was worthy," Lola said. "You know, it's ridiculous in a way, but everywhere I go there's such a real bitter antagonism against the Yankees. Even in Hong Kong. A little man asked me not long ago, 'When will the Yankees not win the pennant?' I said I did not know, perhaps never."

"Nuts to the little man in Hong Kong," Joe said.

"Keeping the Yankees from another pennant is a much more worthy cause than mine was," Lola said. "Mine was sheer vanity, I'm afraid."

"What was your cause?"

"Even if I could tell you, I wouldn't. . . . Don't be grim, Joe. One must live in the moment."

"Why can't you tell me?"

"I just can't. Believe me."

When they reached the bridge, he stopped paddling, letting the canoe slip slowly with the current, his imagination rampant with conjecture, with fear, with grim determination.

"Where does this way go?" Lola asked, pointing downstream.

"I don't know," Joe muttered. "To hell, I think."

"Joe, don't be like that. It goes past Mount Vernon, doesn't it?"

"Lola, will you at least do me the favor of getting off that phony Mount Vernon kick?"

"But it's not phony. I'd love to see Mount Vernon.

Especially at night. Wouldn't it be romantic to go there at night, Joe? In a canoe? They have a little dock— Look out, Joe, we're going to bump!"

Pushing off with the blade, he said, "They have a little dock back at the boathouse, too." And turning the canoe, he began paddling back upstream.

"I haven't helped you much, have I?" she asked presently.

He sighed. "It's not your fault, I suppose."

"I wish I could help you," she said. "Every woman wants to help the man she loves."

"The what?"

Lola laughed softly. "I'm in love with you, Joe. Surely you knew."

For perhaps ten strokes, Joe did not reply, and then he said, "You know that's ridiculous, Lola."

"Not at all," she said. "It's certainly not abnormal. Probably a good sixty per cent of the women in America have a crush on you."

"Well, they're crazy. And besides, you wouldn't have the slightest interest in me if it hadn't been for Applegate."

"Mr. Applegate introduced us, Joe . . ." She looked back at him over her shoulder. "But falling in love with you was my own idea."

"But don't you know who I am?"

"I know you're Joe Hardy. That's all I need to know."

"Don't you know who that woman was standing in the yard the day you drove up?"

"I suppose you're going to say it was your wife," she

said. "But it's not Joe Hardy's wife. That much I know. And that's enough for me."

"Well," he said, "if you're in love with me and want to help me, why don't you tell me what I want to know?"

"About Mr. Applegate's strategy? But Joe, I can't."

"Why can't you?"

"First of all, it's a physical impossibility."

"You mean if you opened your mouth and tried to say the words they wouldn't come out?"

"Yes," she said. "That's about it."

"That's not the truth and you know it, Lola."

"It is the truth, Joe. And furthermore . . . well, I'm in a peculiar position."

"How?"

"Well . . ." She laughed shyly. "Applegate said that after September twenty-first, after it becomes permanent . . . I could . . . have you. I mean, you'd be mine. So naturally, I want you to keep on being Joe Hardy."

"You're a nice kid," he said bitterly.

"I know it sounds terrible, putting it that way," she said.

"It reminds me of a story I read once," Joe said grimly. "The demon says this one can be mine . . ."

"But, Joe, even knowing that I'd lose you . . . I'd tell you if I could. But I can't. I really can't."

"Could you write it?"

"No, I couldn't do that either, and here's another thing. Even if I did tell you how it happened to me, I'm sure that wouldn't do you a bit of good. Applegate's so clever, he never works the same trick twice."

"Okay, okay," Joe said. "So we're going to be sweethearts and burn happily ever after."

"Oh, Joe, don't feel that way. Try to see my position. I had nothing to do with it. And besides . . ." She laughed sympathetically. "Poor Joe. You're so naive in some ways. It doesn't have anything to do with *burning* . . ."

She slid gracefully from the seat and spread herself full length in the bottom of the canoe, adjusting a pillow at his feet, and resting her head on the pillow.

"You're very handsome, Joe Hardy," she said, arching her neck and looking up at him.

"And you're the most beautiful girl in the world," he said bitterly. "The greatest baseball player and the most beautiful girl in a canoe on a beautiful night, and isn't that just too damned sweet?"

But his eyes were drawn involuntarily to her face and he found it beautiful in the faint light of the gibbous moon hanging over Arlington. And when he shifted the paddle to the other side, he was careful not to let it drip on her.

"Joe, please don't be like that," she said. "Look on the bright side."

He grunted. "Where is it?"

"There is a bright side, Joe. When the season ends, we could travel. We could go to Provence. How would you like to go to Provence? It is so beautiful, so civilized there . . ."

"I never heard of it," he said, but he felt himself growing

soft inside. Her eyes were closed now, and her soft hair blew gently about her temples.

"Other ball players . . . they go hunting and things like that in the off season, don't they?" she asked, clasping her hands beneath her head. "We could go to Provence and then when spring training starts next year we could go to Florida. You see, Joe, it is far better than burning. Far better."

And although he continued to paddle, he was looking at her hand, noticing how lightly, how caressingly it rested on the canoe. And it struck him that if he were to kiss her, kiss this girl named Lola, it would be like two people without substance kissing; they were two people who did not exist, floating in a canoe, in darkness and silence, floating toward a gossamer bridge. It was an eerie feeling, and a temptation; it was a cave where he could hide from conscience with perfect respectability.

Lola stretched, reaching repose again with a shiver that coursed the length of her body. Then she was reaching for his hand. "Stop paddling a minute, Joe." Her hand was slim and cool. "Why don't you get down here beside me. There's room. We could just float."

"Float where?" he muttered.

"It doesn't matter," she purred. "To Spain perhaps?"

"That would be quite a feat," he said huskily.

"Yes, a pleasant feat," she said. "Shall we float, Joe?"

He looked down, following the long, slender line of her body. "I'm afraid the canoe might tip over, Lola," he said weakly. "I weigh more than you do."

"We could compensate for that by weight distribution," she said.

He raised his eyes. The lights spanning the river ahead now were those of the Key Bridge, and high off to the right there was a lighted clock in a steeple.

Determinedly, he began to count the lights on the bridge, but he had reached only to seven when he broke off. Raising the paddle, he let the water drip off and then stowed it.

"Darling," she said, as he slid carefully in beside her. "Joe, my darling—Joe, what's the matter?"

"I guess I've changed my mind, Lola," he said, moving back to the stern again, reaching for the paddle. One, two, three vigorous strokes, and as the canoe shot forward again, he completed the job of counting the lights.

For a long while, Lola lay there without speaking, looking up at the stars; and then she said, "That was like being stranded in the traffic jam. Only worse. I suppose I'll have to be content to wait until after September twenty-first."

15

"Hey, Applegate."

Thus in the days that followed did Joe summon the hated presence.

"Hey, App, I want to talk to you."

At times in a trumpeting voice, vibrant with indignation; and at other times a whimper. A plea made from anywhere and everywhere. From his hotel room in the dead of night; from his position in right field, as he hopefully scanned the stands.

But it was as though Applegate had been swallowed up by the face of the earth.

And it was as a zombie that Joe Hardy trod the earth's face during those late August days of the long home stand. As a zombie he played and as a zombie he went through the motions of living.

His nights were torture, filled with feverish dreams in which Lola and Applegate were always with him; the three of them walking on giant balloons along off-balance corridors of a giant cavern which glowed always with a faint, pinkish light. In the morning, there was a newspaper with a box score, telling of fresh exploits of a young, handsome, clean-cut youth named Joe Hardy, whose name was a headline and a household word throughout the length and breadth of the land; Joe Hardy, hailed on street

· 137 ·

corners, recognized by cab drivers, besought by boys'
clubs, by TV shows, even by lady discussion groups. Yet,
in the mornings, it was often a long while before he com-
prehended that this Joe Hardy was himself, the young man
who accepted the newspaper from the bell boy and sat
dully reading it by the window.

Day by day, these box scores chronicled a story long
to be remembered in baseball annals, the brilliant story
of the 1958 Washington Senators. Relentlessly, more relentlessly now than the Yankees at their most sadistic,
the Senators ground down the hapless opposition. Over-
taking first the White Sox, then the Orioles, they entered
second place only seven and a half games behind the
Yankees, and now it seemed only a question of time.

Yet to Joe, his own role had become meaningless, indeed anathema. It was true that he could still find faint
pleasure in noticing the expressions of transport on the
faces of Mr. van Buren and Mr. Welch; he was touched
often by the happiness of the other members of the team.
But the sight of a ball arching from his bat into home-run
territory was now something that sickened him. Still he
could not stop hitting them: no more than he could prevent himself from hitting that ball that had ruined poor
Bobby Schantz's no-hitter.

Lola was still present at each game, always in the same
seat, wearing the same demure, faintly saddened expression. But now he read into the look something more.
About her whole attitude now there was an aspect of
waiting, of patience, and of confidence. She was waiting

until the day she could claim him for her own. Until then she was content to wait; for after all, he realized, she had all the time in the world.

At times, uninvited, a voice asked, would it be so horrible a fate? You could search the world over and never find a woman so beautiful. Look at those guys sitting around her. They're not even watching the ball game.

The hotel room became a place to avoid, and on the nights when afternoon games had been played, he took to walking the streets alone, took to seeking out movie houses. In that year 1958, five still remained in Washington alone; and in one of these Joe sat vacantly, lost in his own thoughts and fears, seldom conscious of what was transpiring on the giant screen.

And then came the night when he found himself not far from the modest suburban house he had heedlessly left so long ago. Recognizing the neighborhood brought a faint lift in spirits and, changing route, he began walking more swiftly. But it was now past midnight and when he reached the old familiar block, the house was dark. All the houses were dark. There was no sign even of Old Man Everett, who habitually chose this hour to water his lawn. For a few moments he stood there, peering at his side porch, trying to pierce through the darkness. Merely to make out its furnishings would help. But he could see clearly only his old rocker, dimly white, ghostlike, a rocker with no one to rock.

He turned aside. Right there he had walked down the pathway, right here the taxi had been waiting, and Applegate had said something about come on, hurry up, the meter's running.

With a heavy heart, Joe turned away.

But the next night he returned, earlier in the evening, and the pain of what he found now was even worse. For the house was filled with light and with gay sound, with the shrieks of women and occasionally the bark of a dog. A dog? Whose dog?

Pacing circumspectly, he caught a glimpse. In the living room, seated about the table, were Bess and her bridge cronies. He saw Bess throw up both hands, a gesture he knew to mean triumph, exultation of some kind. Doubtless, he thought bitterly, she had just completed a bid.

Laughter. Triumph. Bright lights. A dog. On the door of this house there was no crepe.

16 First the Indians, next the Orioles, then the White Sox, and finally the Tigers. That was the order of the western clubs' invasion, and it was on the morning of the next to last game of the Tiger series that Joe Hardy rose early, dressed, had breakfast in the hotel coffee shoppe and hailed a cab.

A few minutes before nine, he walked up the front steps, shoulders resolute, purpose clear in mind. Through the screen door, he could see all the way back to the kitchen, where she stood at the sink, her back and hips broad in a yellow floor-length garment, broken at the waist by the white strings of her apron. Sighing, he knocked.

It was as though he had set an infernal machine in motion. Initially there was a frenzied slipping of clawed pads, seeking traction on a bare floor; then a malevolent growl that ascended into frenzied barking as the little black beast negotiated the short distance from wherever he had been stationed and stood scowling up through the screen door.

"Joe!" Bess called sharply, and he experienced a second of shock before he realized that she was speaking not to him but to the dog. And knowing this evoked shock of a different kind.

Wiping hands on apron, she came toward the door now, saying, "Yes?"

Although in recent years he had seemed to lose awareness of her eyes, he noticed them now, noticed how jolly and kindly they were. Pale blue in color, they lit her face, drew attention from the fleshiness of chin and neck and the gray of her hair. He was struck again by the gentle refinement of her face, its thin, gracefully modeled nose, the pleasant eyes. The garment she wore, he could see now, was her yellow house coat, piped down the front with white lace. How many mornings at the breakfast table had he sat opposite this?

A lump formed in his throat, and he stood, unable to speak.

Bess, he was saying in his mind. *Bess it's Joe. I've come back. I've done a terrible thing. I sold my soul to the devil so the team would win . . . so the Yankees would lose. I thought it would be worth it, but it wasn't. You've got to help me.*

But he looked down at the dog, which still quivered with rage; then back to Bess, and smiled helplessly. And it was then he realized that it must be more than the lump that kept him from speaking.

"What can I do for you?" she asked. It was not a querulous question, but sympathetic, patient.

Still smiling, he raised his hand in a kind of wave of greeting. The dog growled.

"Is it about the room?" Bess asked. And then she said, "Oh, I see. I'm so sorry. I beg your pardon. Would you like to write it?"

And he realized she thought him a mute.

He shook his head.

"You're sure it's not about the room?" she said.

What room? What was she talking about?

But it was then that he spoke, and the words that passed his lips were, "Yes, it's about the room."

In his mind's eye he had a momentary picture of Applegate, in some distant corner of the world, looking his way and pushing a button.

"Oh, certainly," she said. "Now, if you'll just wait until I leash Joe . . ."

In a few seconds she reappeared and opened the screen door for him. He followed her past the living room, where the dog now was leashed to a leg of the sofa, Joe Boyd's sofa, avid eyes upon Joe Hardy, tongue lolling. As they started upstairs, Joe Hardy said, "That's a nice dog. What kind is he?"

"A cocker spaniel," she said. "He wouldn't bite. I leash him because he jumps up on people. He's really very gentle."

"He must be a good watch dog."

"Yes, he's my protector. Now," she went on as they reached the head of the stairs. "As a matter of fact I have two rooms I could show you. . . . This little front room here faces on the street. It's not very big as you can see, but it's a nice little room. My daughter used to sleep there before she was married."

He followed her back down the hall. "And then we have this larger room in the back. This is the one I advertised in the paper." Joe entered behind her, speechless. He looked out the window. Despite the arid summer, she had flowers blooming in back, bordering two sides of the white stucco garage which lay at the foot of the terrace. "This room is larger, of course," she said.

He turned to face her. *Bess, this is ridiculous. I didn't come to rent any room. I'm your husband. Besides, you don't need to rent any rooms. After all that money I mailed you from Boston . . .*

But what he heard himself say was, "This is a wonderful room. How much would this be?"

"This room is eight dollars a week."

"That's fair enough. When would I be able to move in?"

"Now here is the bathroom," she said. "Oh, any time you like. Right away, if you'd like to." She led the way downstairs again, and he followed her into the living room, carefully skirting the dog, which strained at the leash, standing on its hind legs.

"Now remember what I told you, Joe," she said, pointing a warning finger at the dog. "You've got to be decent."

The living room was just as it had always been: the television set, his television set, occupying its accustomed spot between the two front windows; the sofa and two overstuffed chairs arranged to command a view of the screen; her antiques, her bric-a-brac . . .

"Now let me see," she said, laughing apologetically, "I guess there should be some rules I ought to tell you about. . . . The bridge girls said I ought to lay down some rules. . . . You see, I was really thinking more of a lady roomer . . ." She paused, embarrassed.

"I see," Joe said.

"Now if you don't mind, I'd prefer no drinking. Oh, if you'd like to keep a few cans of beer in the refrigerator it would be all right, but . . ."

"I live very quietly," he said.

"And also," she went on, looking away, "no lady visitors in your room, if you don't mind."

"Of course not," Joe said.

"Well," she said brightening, "that's all I can think of. You see, this is kind of new to me. I've never had roomers before, but my husband is away for a while and since I'm rather lonely I thought I'd put the ad in the paper. . . . Oh, there is one more thing." She frowned. "The bridge girls said I ought to ask for references. I hate to ask people for references, so if you would rather not . . ."

"My name is Hardy," he said. "Joe Hardy . . . I'm with the baseball team—"

"Joe Hardy! Well, I'm honored. I thought your face was familiar, Mr. Hardy." She brushed back a wisp of hair, flustered. "Well, I guess that takes care of the references in a hurry."

All trace of the lump in his throat suddenly gone, Joe thought scornfully: *Face looks familiar! How would you know who Joe Hardy is? You don't know second base from the center-field flagpole.*

He asked, "Are you a baseball fan?"

"Oh, yes," she said. ". . . Why are you looking at me like that, Mr. Hardy?" She laughed. "Is it so strange to be a baseball fan?"

"No, of course not," he said.

"To tell you the truth, I didn't use to be," she said. "Once I couldn't stand baseball. Loathed it. It's just rather recently . . . just since my husband's been away, in fact, that I became fond of it." She paused. "Did I say something wrong?"

"Not at all," Joe said.

"You see, my husband is a great baseball fan. I guess he's probably the greatest baseball fan in the whole United States, or close to it, and after he left I had a little talk with myself. I decided that maybe a wife owed it to her husband to develop the same interests he had and so . . ." She smiled. "That's why I did it, because it really used to be a very sore point between us, and I decided it just wasn't fair to him. Some husbands even divorce their wives for less."

Miserably confused by now, Joe stared down at the dog, which lay quiescent finally.

"Besides," Bess went on, "the town's so excited about the team. Even the bridge girls . . . it's rather hard not to get excited too. And we owe it all to you, Mr. Hardy. That's why I can't wait to tell everybody that you're going to room right here in my house. My husband, I know, would be beside himself with excitement if he knew."

She unleashed the dog. Joe sidestepped, but she picked it up and held it to her breast, so that the four legs stuck out at crazy angles. The dog regarded Joe with suspicious eyes, managing a show of ferocity in spite of the undignified position in which it was being held.

"Who's pitching tonight, Mr. Hardy?"

"Ransom, I think," Joe said absently.

"Oh, no, it couldn't be Ransom," she said firmly. "He's only had two days' rest."

He turned to her open-mouthed, but she was examining the dog's ear. "More likely Rocky Pratt," she said. "Or at least I think I'd go with Pratt . . . Well, anyway, will you move in some time today?"

"Yes," Joe said thickly. "Either this afternoon or tonight after the game. I only have a couple of suitcases."

"All right, Mr. Hardy. I'll be expecting you. . . . By the way, I haven't even told you my name. It's Mrs. Boyd . . . Mrs. Joseph Boyd." She laughed. "That makes three Joes. You. My husband. And little Joe here."

Looking mutely from his wife to her dog, he turned then and walked slowly away, holding his eyes on the flagstoned walk, barked all the way to the corner by little Joe, the terrible-tempered cocker: the alter ego, Joe Hardy thought grimly, he had once asked Applegate to provide.

17 The game was over by eleven, and it was just midnight when he arrived, noticing even as he stepped from the taxi that the girls were gathered about the bridge table. He could not help observing sourly that Bess's turn was all too frequent, and this at least was unchanged. It had never been otherwise. Even though the other three had homes, it always seemed to be Bess's turn.

Carrying his suitcases, he walked up the steps to the accompaniment of Joe the dog's barking, somewhere deep within the house. From force of habit, he started to pull open the screen door; thought better of it and raised his knuckles to knock; then entered after all without knocking. Even as a roomer, he had a roomer's right of entry.

"Mr. Hardy, is that you?" It was Bess's voice and, he noticed with disgust, it sounded a shade coy.

"Yes, ma'am," he said, setting down the suitcases. From within the room there was subdued giggling, apropos, so far as he could determine, of nothing. This, too, was normal.

"Would you like to come in for a moment?" Bess called. "I have some ladies who would like to meet you."

And to his surprise, although they were gathered about the bridge table, they were not playing bridge. There were no cards, no tallies in sight.

"Girls," Bess was saying, "I want you to meet Mr. Hardy. Mrs. Kirk, Mrs. Palmer, and Mrs. Buckner."

He smiled and then felt the smile freeze. The very idea was ridiculous. Being introduced to Sara Palmer and Phyllis Kirk and Polly Buckner, when they'd been lousing up his evenings for years.

"Gee, you were wonderful tonight, Mr. Hardy," said Phyllis Kirk, who fancied herself still girlish and who spoke with underlines. "Wasn't he just *won*derful, girls?"

The others chorused variations of agreement, and Bess said, "The girls and I watched you on the TV tonight, Mr. Hardy. Not a speck of bridge did we play all evening . . ."

"Not one single hand," Sara Palmer said.

"That may not sound like much of a sacrifice . . ." Bess said.

"But believe you me . . ." Polly Buckner said.

"It's something we've never done before, ever," Sara Palmer said.

"You were simply wonderful," Phyllis Kirk said.

"Well, thank you," Joe said.

"How you bat the ball so well is beyond me," Polly Buckner said.

"Well . . ." Joe said.

"The whole neighborhood's so excited," Bess said. "Earlier in the evening there were some boys out front, waiting for you to come home. How they found out I'll never know, but I guess news travels fast . . ."

"In a neighborhood like this," Sara Palmer said.

"They had to go home when it got so late," Bess said.

"I guess they had to go to bed," Sara Palmer said.

Sara Palmer had never been one of his favorites.

"We were having a discussion," Bess said. "I counted up that you got four hits, Mr. Hardy."

"And I say three," Phyllis Kirk said.

"Three is right," Joe said. "Where is the dog tonight?"

"See?" Phyllis Kirk said. "Three."

"I have to put him in the kitchen when the girls come," Bess said. "He's . . ."

The four of them giggled.

"Not very gentlemanly," Sara Palmer said.

"Oh," Joe said. "Well, you see, it was only three because one ball I hit got caught."

"Out by the fence," Sara Palmer said.

"That's right," Joe said.

"Mr. Hardy." Polly Buckner produced a scrap of paper and a pencil from her purse. "Would you mind signing this for my son? Just sign 'To Ted Buckner—Joe Hardy.'"

Joe did so, and she said, "I'm afraid Ted's going to be camping on your doorstep. He's so excited."

"And Mr. Hardy," Phyllis Kirk said, "we have a request to make. Could you get the four of us some world-series tickets?"

Joe smiled. "It's a little early for that."

"Oh, but it's certain you're going to win, isn't it?" Phyllis Kirk said.

"You're doing so well," Sara Palmer said.

"The Yankees might have something to say about that," Joe said. "No tickets are on sale yet."

"But would you put in our names, the four of us, so our order will be in?" Phyllis Kirk said.

"Well, yes, I'll be glad to," he said. "Well, it was very nice meeting you ladies."

Bess said, "We're going to have refreshments in a few minutes, Mr. Hardy. Won't you have something?"

"We always have refreshments right at twelve o'clock," Sara Palmer said in explanation, and then laughed heartily.

"That's very kind of you," Joe said, "but I guess I ought to be getting to bed."

"He has to get plenty of sleep so as to knock the ball well, isn't that right, Mr. Hardy?" Polly Buckner said.

"Hit the ball well, you mean," Sara Palmer said. "Knock the ball sounds clumsy."

"Mr. Hardy," Bess said, "I didn't realize, but they said on the TV tonight that you were leaving for Chicago tomorrow night."

"Surely. They go west," Sara Palmer said. "I heard them say the team goes west. The ghost goes west. A movie, wasn't it?" She giggled, and Joe looked at her narrowly.

"Boston first, then Cleveland," he said.

"Then you won't be here for a while," Bess said.

"I guess not," he said.

"Sleep well," they said, as he picked up his suitcases and climbed the stairs.

"It was nice to meet you," Sara Palmer said.

Closing the door firmly behind him, Joe sat on the edge of the bed for a while and looked out the window. His heart was pounding as it might after a long run. Moonlight bathed the back lawn. It had the texture of frost, and to notice this was soothing. From downstairs came a low, sustained flutter of conversation, punctuated at times by shrieks. He smiled faintly. What they were having down there was something in the nature of a tenth inning.

Finally he began to undress and then, as was his habit, headed for the bathroom to change into his pajamas. As he opened the door, the voices below rose up in a wave of sound, and riding the crest was the voice of Sara Palmer, shrilling, "Oh, Bess, molded tuna, my absolute favorite!"

This, he thought, beholding his image, was the first time the face of Joe Hardy had ever appeared in the bathroom mirror of Joe Boyd, and although he had by now grown almost accustomed to the sight of this face, its reflection in this mirror was startling. Looking about, he saw that his shaving articles were nowhere in sight. Not in the medicine cabinet and not in the closet. Bess must have hid them to save face. A normal man who leaves on a normal business trip takes along his shaving articles.

By the time he left the bathroom he was lost deep in thought and from long habit headed automatically for the bedroom he had shared over the years with Bess. He was half way down the hall when a hoarse voice called, "Hey!"

He turned, and although there was no sign of Applegate it was certainly Applegate's voice.

"Hey, Joe, wrong room," it said in a hoarse whisper. "You'd scare her to death if she came up and found a right-fielder in her bed."

Applegate laughed, eminently pleased with his joke.

Joe walked slowly to the back room and turned on the overhead light. No sign of Applegate. He sat on the bed, thinking what a huge joke this must be to Applegate—the dog named Joe; Bess becoming a fan; his being a roomer in his own house. Applegate stopped at nothing. But this time Joe would not whimper or beseech. He had done enough beseeching. It was time for action. Applegate played dirty. But two could play the game.

18 Next morning he heard the clock downstairs strike ten. He opened one eye, thinking that it was like a time, long years before, when he had been sick and had slept alone in this same back room. He remembered the feeling of warmth and security. From deep within the pillow, he had watched the shadows creep across the wall as the sun moved slowly through the long afternoons.

He turned over and went back to sleep.

Later he was wakened by a tap at the door. "Mr. Hardy. It's almost twelve o'clock. The game starts at two-thirty, doesn't it?"

"Yes," Joe said. "Thanks, Mrs. Boyd."

He turned over and went back to sleep.

"Mr. Hardy!" Her voice this time was alarmed. "It's after one o'clock."

"Oh, really?" he said. "Well, I guess I'd better hustle."

"I should say. Is there anything I can do to help you get ready? Would you like some breakfast?"

"No, ma'am. No, thanks. I'll make it."

He smiled, nestling back under the sheet. There was a slight tang in the air, the tang of a late summer day, foretelling autumn.

It couldn't have been more than twenty minutes or so before she was at the door again. This time he didn't answer, and he heard her go away, saying, "Oh dear, oh dear."

Speaking of sleep, he thought, this was the most marvelous sleep he'd had in weeks. No dreams of Applegate, no caverns, no lopsided floors and walls. By now it must be close to game time, he judged, dozing off again. Dimly he seemed to hear Bess's voice from a great distance, explaining, lamenting.

When she returned again, she said, "Mr. Hardy, you're wanted on the telephone."

"How come?" he said. "Who is it?"

"It's Manager van Buren," she said.

"How did he know where I was?"

"I called the ball park office," she said apologetically. "I thought they ought to know you weren't . . . Did I do wrong?"

Joe yawned. "I don't know," he said. "It doesn't matter much, I guess."

"Will you talk to Mr. van Buren?"

"No. Tell him I can't possibly talk to him."

"He sounds upset."

"Tell him I won't be able to make it today."

"But Mr. Hardy, the team needs you. They might lose." Her voice was anguished.

He smiled. "I'm very sleepy," he said. "I don't feel up to snuff exactly."

She sighed and went away.

It was still later, and he had napped again, when she returned. "May I come in, Mr. Hardy?"

Pulling the sheet firmly in place, he said "Okay."

She carried the radio from the side porch. "I thought maybe you'd like to listen to the game," she said, stooping to the outlet. "I'll plug it in for you right here."

She straightened and looked at him with concern. Her cheeks were flushed; somehow she looked younger. "Do you have a fever?" she said.

"I don't think so."

"Mr. van Buren was rather angry," she said. "He was sputtering. He wanted to know what the trouble was."

"What did you tell him?"

"I didn't know quite what to say. He'd been calling some hotel where he thought you were staying. He didn't know you'd moved in here . . . I gave him this address . . . It's already tuned to the right station," she said as the radio came on. "Nobody's touched that radio, I guess, since the last night my husband listened to it. He always listened to the games. He was a great fan."

Her voice caught slightly and she turned away. Then she said, "Would you like me to call a doctor, Mr. Hardy?"

"No, thanks. I'll be all right. I just need a little rest."

"Well, you enjoy yourself and if you want anything just call me." She left, closing the door quietly behind her, but then opened it again. "When does the team leave for Boston?"

"Right after the game," Joe said.

"Well . . ." She looked at him quizzically.

"I won't be going," he said.

"Oh, Mr. *Hardy*. They'll never catch the Yankees."

Joe shrugged. "Maybe I'll be able to join them in a few days or so," he said.

With a final worried look, she closed the door.

Joe smiled and relaxed again. The familiar voice of the play-by-play announcer, the voice he had been listening to for almost twenty years now, filled the room.

"A swing and a miss," it was saying. "And the count on Kuenn goes to one and one-duh . . ." And then, abruptly tense: "Ladies and gentlemen, we've just got word from the bench that Joe Hardy is sick. How bad, we don't know. We do know he's sick and that's why he's not in the starting line-up today. As soon as we get something else we'll pass it right along . . . the next pitch gets the outside corner for a strike, and the count now . . ."

The innings passed, the sun moved, and Joe dozed. He had all but forgotten the pleasure of listening to a baseball game.

This time he was wakened by the frenzied barking of Joe the dog, then was aware of footsteps on the stairs. He came alert in time to hear the announcer say, ". . . and the score at the end of the seventh remains, Tigers six and Senators one. Ladies and gentlemen, it's beginning to look as if the phenomenal winning streak of the Washington Senators is going to end . . ."

And then the tap at the door. "Mr. Hardy," Bess said. "There's someone who'd like to see you."

"Come in."

"Hello, boy, they tell me you're feeling under the weather," a quavering voice said.

It was Adam Welch, shuffling hesitantly forward, impeccably dressed, impeccably groomed to the tip of his snowy goatee. He held out one gnarled hand and Joe took it. "Yes, sir, I don't feel so well," he said, angry at himself that he felt shamefaced.

"You can sit right here, sir," Bess said, setting a chair at bedside. "And I'll leave you two gentlemen alone."

"Well, son," Mr. Welch said, seating himself carefully, "I'm certainly sorry to hear you're under the weather. Certainly sorry . . ."

"It's a bad time to get sick," Joe said, noting the concern in the pale blue eyes. "I'm sorry I couldn't play today."

"Oh, don't worry about that part of it, son." Mr. Welch sat with his hands folded on one knee. "That's not important. I just came out to see if I could do anything for you. I always visit my players when they get sick . . . What's that, son?"

"I said that's a very nice thing for you to do," Joe repeated, already miserable.

"I always do it," Mr. Welch said. "I think it's a club-owner's duty. Now is there anything you need? Anything we could get for you?"

"No, sir, I don't believe so, thanks."

"You won't feel well enough to leave for Boston tonight, of course?"

"I'm afraid not, Mr. Welch," Joe said, concentrating on

the wallpaper, still unable to look the old man in the eye.

The Senators were batting in the seventh.

"Well, you just stay there in bed until you feel better," Mr. Welch said. His hands trembled, Joe noticed, unless he held them securely against his knee. 'There's nothing so important as a man's health. I'm ninety-two years old, Joe, and there's nothing so important as a man's health. Not even winning a ball game."

Joe remained silent, looking again at the wall.

"If you feel like going out to meet the team later, well and good," Mr. Welch said. "But if you don't, that's well and good too."

"Does Benny feel I'm dogging it?" Joe asked.

"Doggin' it nothin'," Mr. Welch said vehemently. "Any manager I hire has to be a human being first of all, and a manager second. Benny gives every player the benefit of the doubt."

They both listened silently as the Tigers' third baseman made a flashy pickup to retire the Senators in the seventh.

"Looks like we might lose today," Mr. Welch said. "But you can't win 'em all. If there's anything I've learned in my life, it's that you can't win 'em all, Joe."

"No sir," Joe said.

With a trembling hand then, Mr. Welch reached into his vest pocket and withdrew a huge gold watch and a heavy chain.

"Joe," he said, "see this watch." He held it up. "See these initials." He pointed to heavily scrolled, concentric initials on the cover. "This watch was given to me by some fans when I was playing ball myself. That was a long time ago. Here, have a look."

Carefully he passed over the watch for Joe's inspection. On the inside cover was an inscription, "To Adam Welch, in gratitude from the fans of Binghamton."

"That watch is one of the prize possessions I own," Mr. Welch said. "It's kept perfect time for over sixty years."

"It's a beautiful watch," Joe said, passing it back.

"No." Mr. Welch paused dramatically, head erect, the upper edge of his goatee moist. "Joe, I want you to keep that watch. In memory of me. Keep it as a token of my appreciation for the happy hours you've given me this summer. You see, I—"

His voice faltered, and he lowered his head. The sun glinted over the snowy hair. "You see, it's time I started passing out a few things anyway," he said, trying to smile. "The doc says I won't be around when spring training starts next year. So, this is my last season." Again he smiled, but his eyes were filled with tears.

"Mr. Welch, I don't deserve this," Joe said. "I appreciate it, sir, but why not give it to some member of your family?"

"Haven't got any family left, son." The old man brushed the sleeve of his jacket against his eyes. "Outlived them all. It was either you or Benny van Buren, and I decided I wanted you to have it because without you . . . the last summer of my life . . . couldn't have been nearly as happy as you've made it."

Mr. Welch rose. "That's mainly why I came out here, Joe.

And to tell you not to move from this bed until you're feeling better. Well, good-bye, son."

And as he left the room, the radio told of the Senators coming up in the eighth, still trailing by five.

Mr. Welch was making his way slowly down the steps, leading always with the same foot, as a child does.

Joe the dog barked, and then the screen door slammed.

Joe Hardy rose slowly from bed and walked to the front bedroom. Through the window he saw Mr. Welch shuffling down the flagstoned walkway toward the car, an elderly car of the electric type: high-domed, seemingly headed in both directions at once. Wearing now a chauffeur's uniform, a man Joe recognized as one of Mr. Welch's pinochle cronies got out and held the door. Mr. Welch climbed in. The car drove away.

Joe looked at the watch, still in his hand; then walked at first slowly, then swiftly, back to his room. Although it was too late now to save today's game, he still had time to get to the station before the train left for Boston.

19 Two could play the game. And yet, in any contest at indecency, how could Joe, or anyone else in the world, best Applegate? If there was hope of survival, it did not lie in any such petty stratagem as refusing to leave his bedroom; it lay rather in keeping his integrity whole, in playing the game as decently as he knew how, in regarding the contract as a document to be respected down to the last comma— in doing all these, even though the party of the other part was one who, however much he might respect its letter, showed the spirit of the contract no respect whatsoever.

But even if decency had not seemed the part of wisdom, of practicability, Joe knew in his heart that he could never have played it dirty, knew it was not in him to play Applegate's game. A man who had always lived a decent life save for one misstep, who had never cheated a client, Joe was fated to live decently still, even to the end of his natural life, which might, he realized, be not far off. Although he objected to the word, it boiled down to a matter of code, and Joe's code gave high importance to the matters of taking one's medicine, of lying in the bed one had made. It was sniveling to do otherwise.

Although it had not been many days since Joe had felt it a matter of no personal concern whether the Senators won or lost the pennant, he cared, and cared deeply. He realized this fact from the second Mr. Welch gave him the watch. To remain rooted in bed would have been derelict in his duty to a group of men whom he had carried to the threshold of immortality. To dump them would have been an unforgivable breach of allegiance to his team mates, good fellows, who had given the big try; to Mr. van Buren, who idolized him; to Mr. Welch, who had given him a gold watch.

There are rare occasions, Joe knew, when a man under the impact of tremendous grief, of very great sorrow, will be purged by the experience, will be elevated to a level of understanding and kindliness never before within his reach. During the bright, crisp days of early September, Joe Hardy came to know what this feeling meant.

No longer moody, no longer aloof, he surpassed himself in goodness to others, not merely by hitting home runs, not merely by incredible catches in the outfield, but by small kindlinesses: by standing patiently for hours to sign autographs; helping the clubhouse boy, the bat boy, at their jobs; by a kindly word to the ground crew. When September twenty-first came, he would give the best fight he knew; if it was not good enough, he would at least have known the meaning of gallantry.

But at night, in bed, sometimes he sobbed . . .

Their winning streak snapped by the Tigers, the Senators rebounded like champions. Taking both ends of the Labor Day doubleheader at Boston, they journeyed west to Cleveland, bopping the Indians three straight; thence to Detroit, where suitable revenge was exacted with four from the Tigers. Doubling back then, they took three in Baltimore, a western city located in an easterly sector; and finally to Chicago, where a victory in the first game extended the new winning streak to thirteen straight. On the morning of the second game, the Senators found themselves only three games back of the Yankees. This was on September fifteenth.

He rose late that morning, and although he took no notice at the time, he was to recall later that the elevator boy's manner was distinctly strange on the trip down to breakfast. No sooner had Joe stepped into the car than he began to cast sidelong glances and several times seemed about to speak, but remained silent.

But the behavior of the elevator boy was nothing compared with what confronted him as he stepped into the lobby. He had taken no more than five steps when he was arrested by the sight of the faces: Faces raised from newspapers. All eyes were upon him. On every face a question. On some sympathy; on some disgust; on all, doubt.

Joe stopped short, his eye caught by a banner headline two inches high. The words stared at him:

STAR BALLPLAYER ACCUSED AS PHONY

His heart leapt up and choked him. His face burned.

JOE HARDY CALLED

HARMFUL TO BASEBALL;

OUSTER RECOMMENDED

Guiltily he looked about the lobby. And although his impulse was to turn and flee, he picked up the paper and read:

"New York, September 14—A noted sports columnist said tonight he is ready to give the Baseball Commissioner indisputable evidence that Joe Hardy, star right-fielder for the Washington Senators, is a 'phony and a poseur' whose continued presence in the lineup is an 'insult to the American League.'

"The accusation was made in a prepared statement by Luster Head, columnist for the New York *Bugle*, who said he has asked the Commissioner to schedule a hearing for the purpose of airing his charges. These are so damaging, the columnist said, as to warrant young Hardy's expulsion from organized baseball.

" 'Hardy is guilty of conduct so insidious as to be almost beyond belief,' Mr. Head's statement said. 'The hoax he has worked on organized baseball makes the Black Sox scandal look pale by comparison.'

"Head stated that young Hardy lied in allegedly saying at a press conference some weeks ago that he is a native of Hannibal, Missouri. Beyond this, the columnist declined to reveal the substance of his charges for the present, but said they were based on personal investigation and on information volunteered by a 'former associate' of the Washington ball club. He did not identify his informant."

Scalp on fire, Joe looked up. From every chair he was being watched. He read on:

"Head said it was 'entirely possible and certainly desirable' that as a result of his findings every game won by the

Senators since young Hardy joined the team would be changed in the league standings to a game lost. The Senators, playing at a phenomenal pace since mid-season, are now in second place, only three games back of the Yankees. Since joining the team in July, Hardy has compiled the fabulous total of 48 home runs, and this in less than two months. His batting average is currently an astronomical .545.

"Head said his interest in the Hardy case was first aroused when the player claimed he never had played organized ball prior to joining the Senators. The columnist also recalled that some weeks ago he challenged publicly whether young Hardy had been born and raised in Hannibal.

"Head said he went personally to Hannibal and there ascertained that 'not one of the populace of that upright city had ever heard of Joe Hardy living there, nor of anyone answering his description who might have taken Joe Hardy as an assumed name.'

" 'When this reporter made that fact known, Hardy brashly belittled it,' Mr. Head's statement continued. 'This reporter then thought it best to wait until the full story was in before making further accusations. The evidence is now in and will be presented to the Commissioner in the interest of keeping baseball a game with clean hands . . .' "

A shadow fell across the page. When Joe looked up there stood Benny van Buren, and although his face was sober it showed no panic. "What is all this stuff, Joe?" he asked quietly. "What's this guy got on you?"

Joe stared at the floor, conscious of the vastness and unnatural quiet of the lobby; conscious too that he must answer, must force words to his lips.

But when they came, they came easily, naturally. "You tell me, Ben," he said evenly. "Then we'll both know. Personally I think the guy's been having nightmares."

"You mean there's nothing to it? Nothing in your past life you're ashamed of?"

"Not a thing, Ben," he said, facing Mr. van Buren's steady gaze. "Not one lousy thing. My hands are clean."

Mr. van Buren expelled his breath with a long, whistling sound and dropped to a sofa.

"My boy," he said, "you've just saved the Chicago River Police a grappling job. Now the question is, can you prove it?"

"Prove it?" Joe demanded. "What am *I* supposed to prove? He's the one making the accusations."

"True enough, but—"

"Did you ever hear anything so fantastic in all your life?" Joe asked, his voice gaining strength.

"Listen, Joe, don't get me wrong. I'm with you one, hundred, per cent. The only thing is, we got a wire from the Commissioner's office saying you're suspended until you can clear yourself. They've scheduled a hearing and you're supposed to be there."

"Okay, so I'll go to the hearing and clear myself, but why

do I have to be suspended while I'm waiting? I thought a guy was supposed to be considered innocent until he was proved guilty."

"Everybody's always scared to death that baseball's going to lose its snow-white reputation again," Mr. van Buren said. "That's why they suspended you, and there's not much we can do about it."

Joe shook his head. "Here I'm supposed to defend myself and I don't even know what the charges are. When is the hearing?"

"It's the twenty-first. Well, there's one specific thing. That business about Hannibal."

"The twenty-*first?*"

"Yeah, listen, Joe, can you show evidence to prove you were raised in Hannibal?"

"Why the twenty-first? Why so long?"

"Well that's . . . what? Six days. That's about normal."

"Okay," Joe said grimly. "So it's the twenty-first."

"The only trouble is the team," Mr. van Buren said. "Look, Joe, I'm not worried so much about you. I know we can ram this thing down Head's throat. What worries me is the team's morale. Some of the guys sound pretty discouraged. I mean when they read that stuff about taking all those games we won away from us. Hell, if that happened we'd be down in the cellar."

"It won't happen, I'll see to that," Joe said, amazed at the forthrightness of his voice.

"Okay, but we gotta convince the boys of that. How about making a little speech to them, Joe? I'll get 'em all together up in my room and you do the necessary. And after that, I think the best thing for all concerned would be for you to beat it back to Washington to wait for the hearing. Do you agree?"

"What happens to the team meanwhile?"

"We'll just have to do the best we can, that's all. That's why I want you to give the guys a little pep talk. Give me about ten minutes and then come on up to the room, Joe."

The room was filled when he arrived. Filled with the men whose faces now were so familiar; faces that showed concern, anxiety, but certainly no ill feeling.

"What did you do, Joe?" somebody asked. "Rob a bank or something?"

"You musta been having dates with that Head guy's wife," somebody else said.

He smiled. These were men waiting to be convinced but willing to give him the benefit of the doubt, and sensing this brought a lump to Joe's throat. The faces blurred. For a second he was forced to turn aside and stare with great intentness at the baseboard. He turned back finally, and then heard his own ringing baritone, too bold, too shamelessly cocksure.

"Fellows, I think you'll agree with me that this is a helluva position to be in. Here I am being accused of something and I don't even know what it is. But there's one thing I can say from the bottom of my heart. Whatever Head's talking about—it's a lie."

There was a stir of relief.

"Next Thursday," he went on, "there's going to be a hearing. I'll be there, and you can bet your life I'm going to ram whatever Head says down his throat. All I ask meanwhile is a little faith. If you want to condemn me after Thursday, okay. I'm sure you won't."

Applause broke out, and there were cries of "You tell 'em, Joe" and "Why don't you slug that guy Head in the teeth?"

Joe held up his hand and was surprised to find it steady. "Meanwhile," he said, "you guys have got a job on your hands. As of this morning, we're three games behind the Yankees. To catch 'em we've gotta keep on playing ball to win. Don't let this thing affect you. Just keep on playing like the finest team in the world—which you are. And now, so long."

He left the room to an ovation. But he was only a few steps down the corridor when he began to shake all over. Mr. van Buren was behind him. "Joe," he said, "wait a minute. Where you going?"

"I don't know. The airport, I guess."

"Look, I'll call you as soon as we get back in town," Mr. van Buren said. "As a matter of fact, I'll fly out of here ahead of the team. Now here's the name of the club's lawyer," he went on, handing over a card. "Call him as soon as you get in town and talk things over with him. He knows his stuff. I'm going to call him myself in a few minutes to tell him you're on your way."

Mr. van Buren held out his hand. "Okay?"

"Okay, Ben. And thanks."

"We believe in you, boy. Just remember that. The team believes in you."

A few minutes before take-off time that afternoon, Joe was staring forlornly out the window when someone dropped heavily into the seat beside him. Joe turned. "Well, if it's not good old slippery Applegate," he said.

"I knew you'd want me near in this moment of crisis," Applegate said, "so I came as soon as I could."

"That was reliable of you," Joe said.

"Do you suppose they'll serve supper on the plane? Joe, what's wrong? Surely you're not blaming me for this, are you?"

"The way I feel now I'm not blaming anybody for anything," Joe said wearily. "I don't care what happens any more. I feel like I'm going to have a nervous breakdown."

"That's no attitude, boy," Applegate said, smiling faintly. "You're in hot water and we've gotta get you out."

"Fasten your seat belt, sir," the stewardess said.

"Oh, sure. I'm sorry. Stewardess, will supper be served on this flight?"

"In about half an hour."

"Good," Applegate said.

The stewardess examined a list. "Mr. Hardy, is that correct? And you are Mr. . . ."

"Applegate."

"And your first name, sir?"

"The initial is M," Applegate said.

"Thank you, sir."

"This would never have happened if you hadn't propositioned Ent that night," Joe said when the stewardess had gone.

"Joe, don't get sore. We won't gain anything by getting sore. Darn! These things make me nervous," Applegate went on as the plane reached the head of the take-off strip. Its engines thundered in preparation. "And Joe, for that matter—"

He broke off, and not until the plane was in the air did he resume, first sighing heavily and saying, "It's the take-offs and landings that get me."

"That's a shame," Joe said.

"Listen, lad, if you hadn't tried to butt in that night with Ent . . . oh, well, we're in this together and instead of squabbling about whose fault it is, let's use our mental energy to better purpose. Do you have any ideas?"

"Yeah. Quit the team and hide somewhere until September twenty-first comes and you change me back. Nuts to the whole mess."

"Joe. Joe. Have you stopped to figure out what that would mean?"

"I don't much care what it would mean at this point."

"Listen, Joe, this should be a challenge to your ingenuity, lad. I must confess that I feel rather stimulated on the whole. Now, look, let's do some thinking. Let's start weeding out possibilities. That's what I always do when I've got a problem. Let's get our starting points all lined up. Now, let's assume you just quit. What happens?"

"You tell me. You're the one who's stimulated."

Applegate looked up expectantly as the stewardess began distributing trays to the passengers in the forward seats. "All right, here's what happens. Let's take its effect on the team first. If you quit and disappear, it's the same thing as admitting guilt. So, every game the team's won will go into the lost column. They drop down to the cellar, right? The Yankees win the pennant, right? Mr. van Buren and Welch and all the others, they're publicly humiliated, right? Am I right?"

"Yes, you're right."

"Old Man Welch dies with a bitter memory in his heart and his team in the cellar. In fact I wouldn't be surprised if it killed him on the spot. I should think that would be enough right there to convince you. Don't you have any sensibilities left?"

"You can't expect everybody to be as sensitive as you are, Applegate."

"Look, Joe," Applegate said, unperturbed, "no matter what else happens, no matter whether you decide you want to go on being Joe Hardy the rest of your life or return to Joe Boyd—I think you owe it to all concerned to show up at that hearing and defend yourself . . . a-a-a-h, here we are. Thank you, madam."

As their suppers were set before them, he said, "It looks very tasty, very tasty indeed. You know," he went on in a confidential tone as the stewardess left, "I really don't see how these airlines manage so well with food. Look at that. Steak. In midair."

"I never saw anybody think about his stomach as much as you do," Joe said.

"A man's got to eat," Applegate said, sipping from a plastic cup of tomato juice. "Now, look Joe. Here's another thing. Say you quit and run off. That means your entire summer is wasted, right? Not one thing accomplished. In fact you'd be leaving the team worse off than when you found it. . . . Now let's not get panicky. . . . Use your head . . . Aren't you going to eat?" Applegate asked, flourishing his own knife and fork over the steak.

"I'm not hungry."

"Well, do you agree that defending yourself at the hearing is your first objective?"

"Listen," Joe said, "you seem to forget that I'm not nearly so worried about the hearing as I am about what happens to me after the hearing."

"You mean you're still set on switching back to Joe Boyd again, is that it?"

"Yeah, that's it."

Applegate grunted. "I thought living at home a few days might change your mind. I see now I could have saved you the trouble."

"It was no trouble," Joe said grimly. "I enjoyed it."

"Incidentally, Joe, I thought it was rather touching—you trying to stay in your bedroom instead of playing ball." Applegate grinned. "You found out the good old American game was still in your bloodstream, eh, boy?"

Joe remained silent, looking out at the clouds.

"So you want to switch back to Joe Boyd," Applegate said, his mouth full. "I never thought I'd see the day. Why do you want to switch back? I think you'd be crazy to switch back."

"It just happens that I want to switch back, that's all."

"I don't understand it," Applegate said, shaking his head. "Look. Stay Joe Hardy, and what happens? You're a heroic baseball player for years to come. The team rides high for years to come. You spend your winters in vacation spots. Lola's happy. Van Buren's happy. Maybe Old Man Welch's life gets prolonged. Head gets his come-uppance. I'm happy. Everybody's happy."

"How about my wife?"

"Stop speaking of her as your wife, will you?" Applegate demanded. "She's not your wife now, and hasn't been for weeks. Listen, are you going to eat that steak or aren't you?"

Applegate's eyes were avid.

"Here, take it and be even happier," Joe said.

"Thanks," Applegate said, making the transfer. "It's tender as butter. Well, anyway, let's talk about the hearing. Let's see, it's the twenty-first, isn't it? The same day your contract expires."

"Which in itself seems quite a coincidence."

"Yes, it does for a fact," Applegate said.

"I'm going to ask the Commissioner personally to move the date up," Joe said.

"No, don't do that, Joe. In the first place, I'll need all that time to get my case in order."

"What do you mean, get your case in order?"

"Well, I'm going to be your lawyer, of course."

"You!"

"Certainly me. Who else?"

"The club lawyer."

"Don't be silly, Joe. I'm the man to defend you. Not some stupid, fumbling idiot of a club lawyer."

"Van Buren won't stand for you being the lawyer."

"You tell him you insist on it. Tell him I'm a close personal friend."

"I'm still going to have the hearing moved up."

"No, Joe, I need the time, and furthermore it really doesn't make so much difference that they both fall on the same day. I mean, I wouldn't switch you back until night falls anyway, because that's when I do all that sort of thing."

Joe dabbled at his fruit cocktail.

"Listen," he said, "is this Head guy serious? Is he actually going to try and tell the Commissioner about *us*? Nobody would believe him. People would laugh at him."

"Maybe he's got something entirely different in mind," Applegate said. "Something else on you."

"Like what?"

"I don't know. I can't read Luster Head's mind. But maybe it's not about us at all. The point is, though, we've got to be prepared for the worst. . . . Now, look, Joe, as soon as I finish eating I'm going to pull out. There's no time to lose. What I've got to do is get away to some quiet place and get the old bean to working . . ."

"How about Ent? If you show up at the hearing, he'll recognize you."

"Leave Ent to me. Now first of all, I don't think you should go back to your own house—Boyd's house, that is—before the hearing. I mean, after all . . . the stuff in the papers and all. Okay?"

"Okay," Joe said wearily. "What else can I say but okay? You're running it."

"Right. Just lie low in the hotel. And I'll be at the hearing bright and early on the twenty-first. You know, I'm kinda looking forward to this thing. I have my advocates, of course, but it's not often the old man gets a chance to plead a case personally."

Applegate stood, swaying a little with the motion of the plane. "You can trust me, Joe."

"I'd like to think so."

Applegate smiled. "Look at it this way, Joe. Who else have you got to trust? I'm the one who can clear you. I'm also the guy who switches you back."

He turned and walked down the aisle. Joe saw him enter the door marked MEN — HOMMES and saw him no more that day.

21 "And so, Mr. Commissioner," Luster Head said, "since it appears my principal witness in this case has been delayed, I move the hearing be held over until tomorrow afternoon at three o'clock."

Applegate, seated next to Joe at the defense table, consulted his watch. It was then almost six-thirty. "That's out," he whispered. "That's out, Joe. Right?" Joe nodded grimly.

"Mr. Commissioner," Applegate said, rising and walking toward the dais where the Commissioner sat, flanked by the president of each league. "Mr. Commissioner, I submit that such a delay would be unconscionable."

Pausing, he turned dramatically toward the overflow crowd, adjusting the lapels of his double-breasted dark blue jacket. With this, he wore white flannel trousers, making his appearance more nautical than barristerial, although in poise and forensics he had been most impressive throughout.

"Mr. Commissioner," Applegate went on, "my client, Mr. Hardy, has undergone untold mental anguish for the better part of a week now. He stands ready to defend himself. The hearing was set for September twenty-first, sir, and I submit that on September twenty-first it should be held. I say to you that even another twenty-four hours of anxiety for my client would be unnecessary and extreme cruelty."

Again he paused. The crowd stirred. Joe examined the backs of his hands, then looked up at Mr. Welch and Mr. van Buren, seated side by side in the front row. Mr. van Buren raised a clenched fist, a gesture of encouragement, and Mr. Welch followed suit.

"And Mr. Commissioner, furthermore," Applegate continued, "I should like to call to the Commissioner's attention the fact that this hearing has now been going on since the hour of three, and that so far Mr. Head has declined even to state the specific nature of his accusation. He has resorted only to the very vague contention that Mr. Hardy has been guilty of conduct harmful to organized baseball, and even for this charge he has adduced absolutely no evidence beyond a statement from the Recorder of Deeds in the town of Hannibal, Missouri, and a few letters from residents of that city, purporting to show that Mr. Hardy was never born there. Beyond this, Mr. Head has confined his case, if case it may be called, to a continued harping on the thesis that baseball is and has always been a clean game. He has further emphasized what he considers the injustice of a situation which finds the New York Yankees in jeopardy of losing the pennant."

Applegate's face broke into a smile, and his voice became heavy with irony. "Mr. Commissioner," he said, "it might almost appear that in the opinion of Mr. Head, anything harmful to the Yankees is also harmful to baseball—automatically unclean, *per se*."

The hearing was being held in a banquet room of the leading Washington hotel, and at this thrust the heavily partisan crowd rippled with laughter, then applauded. The Commissioner sounded his gavel, and Applegate went on.

"Now, Mr. Commissioner, the defense does not dispute that baseball is and should remain a clean game. As the Great American Sport, it has no place for misconduct. But Mr. Commissioner, I submit that emphasizing and re-emphasizing the cleanliness of baseball is not, strictly speaking, the purpose of this hearing. The purpose of this hearing is to examine the nature of Mr. Head's accusation and to hear his supporting evidence. And since, in over three hours' time, Mr. Head has done little but shillyshally, I respectfully move, Mr. Commissioner, that for lack of evidence the case be dismissed and my client summarily cleared."

Amid great applause, Applegate walked gravely back to the table and sat down. "How was that, boy?" he whispered. Joe grunted, his eye on the Commissioner, who was conferring with the two presidents. The three of them were comparing watches. Then the Commissioner asked, "Mr. Head, what time was your witness to have been here?"

"At three o'clock, sir. I know of no reason for the delay, although," and Head turned toward Joe, "considering the character of the defense, it's not inconceivable that my witness may have met foul play."

Applegate rose swiftly, saying, "Mr. Commissioner, I submit that Mr. Head's remark was completely uncalled for."

"I agree, Mr. Applegate," the Commissioner said. "Mr.

Head, in the future, kindly refrain from gratuitously maligning counsel or defendant." Again he ducked his head in consultation, then intoned:

"Mr. Head's motion for postponement is denied. Mr. Applegate's motion for dismissal is also denied."

"In that case, Mr. Commissioner," Applegate said, "May I suggest in view of the hour that proceedings be recessed for a supper period of reasonable duration."

"Good idea, Mr. Applegate." The Commissioner consulted his watch again and the presidents did likewise. "It is now a quarter to seven. The hearing stands recessed until eight-thirty." The Commissioner sounded his gavel and rose.

"Well . . ." Applegate sat down again, assembling a sheaf of papers as the humming audience began to move out. "You can't say I'm not doing my best for you, lad. Shall we get something to eat? Gentlemen . . ." he said, rising with a courtly bow as Mr. van Buren and Mr. Welch approached. "How does it seem to be going? Will you join us for supper?"

"Mr. Hardy . . ." The familiar voice; the very familiar voice. Then he saw her, pushing her way through the crowd, wearing the blue dress she sometimes wore to church, and a new blue hat with a rose on it.

"Mr. Hardy, I just wanted you to know that I'm rooting for you, and so are the other girls."

She reached his side, laying a hand on his arm, but he could not meet her eyes. Applegate looked at them curiously.

"Mrs. Boyd," Joe said with an uneasiness far greater than he had felt even on the day he had taken the room. "I'd like you to meet Mr. Welch, Mr. van Buren, . . . and this is Mr. Applegate. Mrs. Boyd . . . is my landlady."

"Yes, I've met Mrs. Boyd," Mr. Welch said. "She has the little dog."

"That's right," Bess said smiling. Had her face always been so animated? "Well, I won't keep you, but I did want you to know we were with you. And the very best of luck, Mr. Hardy."

She moved away then, a familiar figure in a light blue dress, and Joe followed her with his eyes until she reached a companion he recognized as Sara Palmer, who waved and blew him a kiss. Even then he continued to watch until they had disappeared into the crowd.

"That's a very attractive landlady you have, Joe," Applegate said, the corner of his mouth twitching in amusement. "Well, gentlemen, shall we eat?"

At supper, Applegate completely monopolized the conversation, first going over with Mr. Welch and Mr. van Buren the ground he would cover when he put them on the stand, and afterward telling anecdote after anecdote about his experiences on a dude ranch in Wyoming, experiences which Joe was confident were fictitious, but their telling aroused in him neither interest nor resentment. While Mr. van Buren and Mr. Welch laughed in appreciation, he ate dully, taking no pleasure in the meal which, it occurred to him just before dessert came, might very likely be the last he ever ate as a . . . what? He could not answer and, stirring uneasily, looked at his watch. It was seven-thirty.

Nor, after the hearing resumed with Head's star witness still absent, could Joe muster any real interest in the testimony itself, although it was now testimony resoundingly favorable to the defense. Somberly, and with frequent glances at Bess, he heard his own character eulogized, first by Mr. van Buren and now by Mr. Welch who, sitting alertly erect in the witness chair, his feet not quite reaching the floor, was just concluding to a hushed room:

"Man and boy, I've been in the game of baseball. It's been my whole life, and never have I seen a young man with finer qualities than young Joe Hardy. Mr. Commissioner, I'm opposed to corruption in baseball just as much as the next fellow. My record will show that. But I think it's a sin and a shame for any young fellow to have his name dragged in the dirt for no reason, the way this poor boy's has been. A sin and a shame!"

Getting with difficulty to his feet, Mr. Welch shook his finger at Head, as he had done once many weeks before at the press conference. "Mr. Commissioner, if this fellow Head thinks there's dirty business afoot in the American League, why don't we investigate the New York Yankees? They're the ones who've won the pennant all these years. Not us. Not Chicago. Not Cleveland. But the Yankees." The silvered head bobbed in emphasis as the cheers began. "Mr. Commissioner, if you want my opinion, this fellow Head doesn't have any case at all. Luster Head just wanted to get Joe suspended so he couldn't play ball for us. And I call that a dirty rotten trick. I thank you."

It was several minutes before order could be restored in the hearing room. While the Commissioner futilely sounded his gavel, Mr. Welch walked with shining eyes over to the defense table, where Applegate clasped his hand warmly. With flushed face, the old man accepted the gabardine coat which his chauffeur held for him; then, making ready to leave, turned to Joe.

"Son," he said, "I've got to get home to bed now. I'm sorry I can't stay until the end, but I know just as sure as you're living that when I wake up in the morning I'm going to read in the papers that your good name has been cleared."

A fresh burst of applause broke out as he left the room.

"Mr. Commissioner," Applegate said, moving toward the dais. "Mr. Commissioner . . ." Turning to the audience, he raised a hand and the hubbub gradually faded. "Mr. Commissioner, it is now nearing the hour of ten. Before we proceed, I should like to put a question to Mr. Head. Mr. Head, I ask you, where is your witness?"

"I expect him at any minute," Luster Head replied coolly.

"Mr. Commissioner," Applegate said, "ever since we returned from the supper recess, Mr. Head has been saying that he expects his witness at any minute. He is still absent. Once more I move for dismissal of this ridiculous case against my client."

"Mr. Applegate, I agree that your motion has merit." The Commissioner paused, rotating his gavel, and Joe felt his heart bound with hope. "But in view of the fact that Mr. Head's entire case appears to rest on the testimony of this single witness, I feel very strongly that he should be given every chance to bring him to the stand. For this reason, I must again deny your motion and ask you to proceed with the case for the defense."

"Very well, sir. May I ask a few seconds' delay?"

When it was granted, Applegate dropped into a chair beside Joe. "Well, lad . . ."

Joe shook his head grimly. "I'm telling you one thing. Whether it's over or not, we're leaving here at quarter of twelve."

"Oh, absolutely," Applegate said. "Well . . ." He sighed heavily and poured himself a glass of water from the pitcher on the table. "Let's get on with it."

Striding once more toward the dais, he said, "Mr. Commissioner, as I believe I indicated once before, the defense feels it is working somewhat in the dark here. At this point, some five hours after the hearing began, we still have nothing more concrete to chew on than Mr. Head's so-called evidence on the subject of Hannibal, Missouri. Now Mr. Commissioner, first and foremost, I submit that it is no crime not to have been born and raised in Hannibal, Missouri." Applegate chuckled. "Many people were not born and raised in Hannibal, Missouri. I among them. And you, I daresay, Mr. Commissioner, and Messrs. the Presidents. Now then . . ."

Applegate paused, returning to the table for another glass of water. Setting the glass down, he winked surreptitiously at Joe, who grimaced with disgust.

"Be that as it may," Applegate continued, "the evidence concerning Hannibal is all we have before us, and so the defense will now turn its attention to Hannibal—with the simple intent of showing you gentlemen the length to which Mr. Head's desperation has driven him . . . I should like to call to the stand Mr. Paul Wilkerson."

Surprised, Joe glanced from his watch to a spot halfway back in the audience, where a gray-haired man in a white suit was rising, making his way to the witness stand.

"Now Mr. Wilkerson," Applegate began, "I should like to ask you a few questions, and you are to reply, of course, in strict conformity with the truth. Mr. Wilkerson, where is your home?"

"Just outside of Hannibal, Missouri," the witness replied. "About four-tenths of a mile past the city limits."

"And how long have you resided there, sir?"

"Thirty-five years."

"All right, sir. Now tell me, Mr. Wilkerson. Seated over there at the defense table is a young man with sandy hair. Do you know that young man?"

"Sure. That's Joe Hardy."

Luster Head was staring, his white pipe hanging in his fingers six inches from his mouth.

"And how long have you known Mr. Hardy?"

"Ever since he was a baby, I expect."

"And was Mr. Hardy, to your certain knowledge, born and raised in the city of Hannibal?"

"Oh sure. Born and raised."

"And Mr. Wilkerson, did you ever know Mr. Hardy to play baseball in or around Hannibal?"

"Oh sure. He always liked baseball."

"How would you describe Mr. Hardy as a baseball player? Do you know enough of the game to tell us whether he was talented?"

"Talented? I'll say he was talented. He could always hit 'em a mile, even when he was a young kid."

"All right, Mr. Wilkerson. Thank you very much."

This time there was stamping of feet among some members of the audience, as well as shrill whistling and loud cheering. Applegate stood triumphantly, one hand in the side pocket of his jacket, the other resting easily on the arm of the witness chair.

"I should now like to call to the stand Mr. Rodney Birdsell," he said.

"Just a second." Luster Head, face flushed, strode toward the dais. "Mr. Commissioner, I should like the opportunity to cross examine Mr. Wilkerson."

Applegate shrugged. "Your witness," he said.

"Granted, Mr. Head," the Commissioner said.

"Now Mr. Wilkerson," Head began, "what evidence can you give to support your belief that Mr. Hardy was born in Hannibal?"

"Evidence?" Mr. Wilkerson sniffed contemptuously. "I don't need evidence. I just know it, that's all. The night he was born, didn't I sit up all night with his father, right in the next room? He wasn't born until six o'clock in the morning."

"His father?"

"Sure his father. Old Bob Hardy was his father. One of the very best friends I had in the world. When he died, I cried like a baby."

"Mr. Wilkerson," Head said, "what evidence can you give us that you are in fact a resident of Hannibal, Missouri?"

"I can show you the house I live in if you want to go out there and see it." As the audience laughed, Mr. Wilkerson smiled in self-appreciation. "Or I can give you my telephone number and you can call up my wife if you want to. She's sitting home right now."

Head looked steadfastly at the witness, seemed about to speak, then turned away. "That's all, Mr. Commissioner," he said grimly.

"And now," Applegate said, "again I should like to call Mr. Rodney Birdsell."

After Mr. Birdsell there were five more, two housewives and three husbandmen, all of Hannibal. All told of knowing Joe Hardy from childhood; all testified to his natural talent as a ball player.

As for Joe, what at first was surprise and grudging admiration, passed quickly into anxiety and worse as the clock moved on, as the interminable questions and answers continued. By the time the last witness took the stand, it was nearing eleven. He poured another glass of water, although already he had drunk so much that the inside of his mouth felt puckered. His nerves tingled, shot upward through his body into his scalp, and he felt impelled toward the ceiling.

But he sat, sipping the water, staring now at his watch, now at Bess, now at the witness—and at Applegate . . . Applegate, still suave—still, after the long ordeal, looking fresh as a daisy.

And when the last Hannibalite left the stand, Applegate turned to the Commissioner and again moved for dismissal. Joe watched the Commissioner's face, studied it for every nuance, noted with hope that it looked tired as he conferred once more with the two league presidents, then nodded his head several times.

"I think this may be it, Joe," Applegate whispered. "Stop worrying, boy, I think this is it."

The Commissioner sounded his gavel, then turned back to the two presidents. Once more he sounded his gavel. When quiet was restored, he said, "Now Mr. Head, it is the opinion of the hearing body that you have been given ample opportunity to produce—where *is* Mr. Head?"

Joe slumped back. Applegate craned his neck. Head was missing.

"Mr. Head was called to the telephone, sir," somebody at the prosecution table said.

The Commissioner set down his gavel and shrugged wearily, then glanced up as Head hurried into the room.

"Mr. Commissioner!" Head's face was bright with hope. "Mr. Commissioner, I have just had a telephone call from my witness. He is on the outskirts of the city and will be here within twenty minutes."

Joe groaned. The Commissioner toyed with his gavel.

"Well, all right, Mr. Head," he said finally. "We've waited this long. I suppose we can wait another twenty minutes. Where has your witness been?"

"His bus broke down soon after they left Pocomoke."

"Very well, Mr. Head. However, it is the feeling of this hearing body that if your witness should not be here in, let us say, thirty minutes—"

"I'm sure he'll be here by that time," Head said.

"Very well. We'll give him until a quarter of twelve. And now while waiting we will have a short recess. We will reconvene at eleven-thirty."

"Come on out in the hall with me a minute," Joe muttered to Applegate.

"Now," Joe said when they were outside. "At ten minutes of twelve, we're leaving. I don't care who's on the stand or whether the Commissioner is standing on his head. We're leaving. Is that understood?"

"Sure," Applegate said. He sighed. "I haven't been through a day like this in a long time. Let me have one of your cigarettes, will you Joe? Thanks. Well, there's this about it, though. Frankly, I think if Roscoe gets here as late as ten of and finishes by, say, five of, we can still swing it easily."

"No, that's cutting it too thin," Joe said.

"You're the doctor, but it doesn't take a second," Applegate said. "Even if we got outside by two minutes of, I could say the word and all of a sudden you'd be old Joe Boyd, heading for the elevator." He dragged speculatively on the cigarette. "Joe, did you ever stop to think, though . . . I mean you're cleared, and then the next minute you disappear. Joe Hardy disappears. How's that going to look from the Commissioner's viewpoint? And the fans'?"

"Who cares?"

"Well, maybe you're right at that. If Joe Hardy has disappeared, they can't bring him to trial again, that's certain."

"For that matter," Joe said, "how about all those phony witnesses? What's going to happen when people out in Hannibal—"

"They're not phony, Joe. Not in the slightest. It's true that if there was ever a vote on whether Joe Hardy once lived in Hannibal there'd be a rather sharp division of opinion among the townspeople but . . . we'd have our supporters, boy, we'd have our supporters."

Joe shook his head in amazement, tinged with disgust. "And what's this stuff about Ent? What's he doing in Pocomoke?"

"It's news to me," Applegate said.

"And what are you going to do when he recognizes you?"

"Just try to bluff it through, I suppose," Applegate said. "It's going to take some bluffing."

"You can say that again. Well, shall we go back in now?"

And as they headed down the hall again, Applegate said in a low voice, "Joe, it breaks my heart to think that in another fifteen minutes or so we'll be saying good-bye."

"I can't say it breaks my heart."

"I refuse to take that personally," Applegate said.

While Applegate went up to converse with the stenotype reporter, Joe made it his first order of business to move both their chairs to the end of the table nearest the exit. Then he sat down to wait.

Promptly at eleven-thirty, the Commissioner and presidents resumed their seats. The hearing room grew still.

"We shall now wait," the Commissioner said.

Luster Head lit and relit his white pipe, glanced at his watch, began to fidget.

At twenty-five minutes of twelve, Applegate called out, "It is now twenty-five minutes of, Mr. Commissioner."

Luster Head rose. "Mr. Commissioner. While we are waiting for my witness I should like to say a few words of preamble to his testimony."

"Very well, Mr. Head. Proceed."

Deliberately, Head relit his pipe and walked slowly to the dais. "Initially, sir," he said, "I should like to make a few remarks about, shall we say, the limits of athletic ability. Now, Mr. Commissioner, as we all know, Babe Ruth set an all-time record for home runs with sixty during the season of 1927. Likewise we know that very rarely in the history of baseball has a player compiled a season batting average of over four hundred. It's been done, of course, but rarely."

Head paused, squared his shoulders and gestured toward Joe with his pipe. "Yet, Mr. Commissioner, here is a man who has hit forty-eight home runs. Not in a full season, but in less than two months. That same man has compiled a batting average of five-forty-five to date. That same man makes phenomenal catches in the outfield. Now, Mr. Commissioner, I ask you, isn't this enough to give a person pause? Does it not seem strange that a man of such incredible skill should have arrived in the major leagues from nowhere—without previous experience in organized baseball, with a past history that is at best vague? Does it not seem, shall we say, peculiar that such a fantastic man should have been all but totally unknown to the world before he suddenly appeared in the outfield of the Washington Senators? What is this mysterious past that makes such an inhumanly perfect ballplayer so mysterious? On the face of it, isn't there reason to find this man suspect?"

Head walked over to the water pitcher and slowly filled his glass. There was a murmur from the spectators and an uneasy stir.

"It's almost twenty minutes of twelve, Mr. Commissioner," Applegate called.

"I have a watch, Mr. Applegate," Head snapped. "Now as for the town of Hannibal, and the witnesses brought to the stand by the defense, I really don't know quite what to say. I can say this. I went personally to Hannibal and searched the court records, and I returned with an affidavit from the Recorder of Vital Statistics showing that no one named Joe Hardy was ever born there. And I made a personal canvass of the townspeople. But for the moment, suppose we leave Hannibal out of this discussion—"

"That's a wise decision," Applegate said, "in view of the circumstances."

"Mr. Applegate, please refrain," the Commissioner said, banging his gavel.

"Suppose," Head went on, "we look instead at the matter of the record book . . . at the records I have just discussed. And at the totals posted in two months of the 1958 season by Mr. Hardy."

Head turned from the Commissioner and faced the audience. "Ladies and gentlemen . . . Mr. Hardy's performance would be startling enough as it stands. But how much more startling, even frightening, does it become when we consider Mr. Hardy's past experience! This man did not rise through the minor leagues. He was not brought along step by step, as a young player might be advanced through the Yankee organization. What was his past experience? Sandlot ball! He would have us believe that he stepped directly from the sandlots into the major leagues . . . that with no past experience he proceeded to perform batting feats undreamed of! Ladies and gentlemen . . . Mr. Commissioner . . . I appeal to you . . . isn't all this enough to make you wonder what manner of man sits before us? Who, really, is Joe Hardy?"

Joe looked furtively about the room, found Bess, who was staring intently at Luster Head. Applegate was smiling.

Dramatically now, Head lowered his voice. "Ladies and gentlemen . . . Mr. Commissioner . . . Messrs. the Presidents, I myself cannot answer that question. I have a theory . . . I have a strong suspicion . . . but I would prefer that you make your own judgment. I would prefer that you hear from the lips of my witness the story that he told me . . . a story profoundly frightening . . . deeply shocking . . . a story—"

The door swung open and in walked Roscoe Ent, followed closely by a slim dark girl with a lithe way of walking.

"Ladies and gentlemen," Head said. "My witness."

Roscoe laughed apologetically. "Better late than never," he said.

"Mr. Roscoe *Ent*," Head said, hurrying forward in greeting.

It was a Roscoe new to Joe. A Roscoe dressed with extreme conservatism in a brown business suit, although, Joe noted, there was nothing conservative about the cut of the black dress worn by the girl with him. She was led to the prosecution table by Head, who then turned and motioned Roscoe to the witness stand.

By Joe's watch, it was exactly twelve minutes of twelve as Head began. "Now, Mr. Ent," he said, face confident, "we haven't a great deal of time, so I must ask these questions rather hurriedly. First, will you identify yourself?"

"I am Roscoe Ent of Pocomoke, Maryland," Ent said, fixing his eyes on the girl.

"Were you formerly employed by the Washington baseball club?"

"Yes sir."

"In what capacity?"

"As an entertainer and part-time pitcher. I helped attendance."

"Very well," Head said, rubbing his hands. "Now Mr. Ent, is that young man at the defense table known to you?"

"Yes sir. That's Joe Hardy."

"Very well. Now Mr. Ent, will you tell the hearing about a recent incident in Baltimore involving Mr. Hardy?"

"Well, I was doing an act in a night club when Joe came over to see me and apologize because I'd lost my job."

"Yes. Proceed."

It was eleven minutes of twelve.

"You mean what happened?"

"Yes, what happened?"

Ent smiled and spread his hands. "That's about all."

Head slowly removed the pipe from his mouth. "What!" he bellowed. The audience hummed. The Commissioner banged his gavel.

"What do you mean that's all, Mr. Ent? How about the man you saw?"

"Oh, that." Ent smiled again. "Yes, there was a man. Joe and I had left the night club, see? When this guy comes up to me and he says, 'Hey, buddy, haven't I seen you some place before?' And I say to him, 'I don't know, have you?' And he says, 'Yeah, wasn't you out with my sister last night?' And I says, 'I didn't know you even had a sister,' and he says, 'I haven't.' Then he nodded and walked off."

From the audience there was an outburst of laughter such as Roscoe had never received at The Dirty Room.

"Mr. Ent," Head demanded in a choked voice, "what are you talking about?"

"That must have been the guy you're thinking of," Ent went on. "I remember saying to Joe that I'd never seen the guy before in my life. And I remember Joe said that guy looks drunk as the devil."

Applegate was chuckling with vast amusement. "It's rich, isn't it, lad?" he said to Joe. "Isn't it rich though?"

"Mr. Ent!" Head pounded fist into palm. "That is *not* the story you told me ten days ago."

"Sure," Roscoe said, unruffled. "It's the same. Oh, maybe not word for word, but just about the same."

"It's ten of, Joe," Applegate said. "Shall we go?"

"Just a second," Joe said.

Head dropped into a chair at the prosecution table and let his head fall slowly over against his clenched hands.

"Mr. Ent," the Commissioner said, "are you familiar with the charge against Mr. Hardy?"

"Bad for baseball or something like that," Ent said. "I'm supposed to be a character witness. Joe's a good boy, a boy with a conscience. He was sorry I'd lost my job . . . I appreciated that. Say, I'm sorry I was so late, Mr. Commissioner, but a couple of fellows turned up sick at the factory and I couldn't get away. Then the bus broke down."

"All right, Mr. Ent. Now Mr. Applegate, I assume there is no need to cross examine."

"None whatsoever," Applegate said, grinning.

"All right, Mr. Ent. You are excused."

Ent grinned. "It was a long trip just for this."

"We owe you an apology, Mr. Ent. Now, Mr. Head, would you mind stepping up here a second please?"

Head strode to the dais, shouting, "Mr. Commissioner, I submit that this man perjured himself."

"Mr. Head, were there witnesses to your purported conversation with Mr. Ent?"

"No, but . . ."

"Well now, Mr. Head," the Commissioner said bitingly, "after all, he was *your* witness . . . you summoned him . . ."

"Okay," Joe whispered. "Now."

"Right," Applegate said, getting to his feet.

And, Joe thought, although the risk had been great, although he had shaved it thin, and although Ent's testimony was inexplicably fantastic, it had all worked out. He had saved the team, saved its victories intact, saved its chance for the pennant, saved it from shame, and there were still eight minutes. And as he headed for the exit, it was with a tiny twinge of regret and nostalgia that he realized that in another few seconds he would be saying good-bye forever to the person of Joe Hardy.

"Just a minute," the Commissioner shouted. "Where does the defense think it is going?"

Joe and Applegate turned.

"We assumed, sir," Applegate said, "that the testimony of Mr. Ent would end the matter. There is obviously no substance for Mr. Head's case. He is obviously a man demented by desperation."

"Be that as it may," the Commissioner said, "the hearing is still in progress. Mr. Hardy, would you take the witness stand, please?"

Joe hesitated, looking at his watch. Seven minutes of.

"It's up to you, lad," Applegate whispered. "I'm ready to do whatever you say."

Quickly Joe strode to the stand.

"Will it take long, sir?" he asked.

"What's the trouble, Mr. Hardy? Am I keeping you from an engagement of some kind? No one has been dismissed. Now, Mr. Hardy, answer if you will, please. What is your home town?"

"Hannibal, Missouri, sir."

"Before joining the Washington club, what was your previous baseball experience?"

"Only sandlot ball, sir."

"Mr. Hardy, do you know of any reason why you are not morally and spiritually qualified to play in organized baseball?"

"None whatsoever, sir."

The Commissioner banged his gavel decisively. "Very well, for the moment. . . . Now, Mr. Head, you mentioned earlier that you had a theory. Do you care to propound that theory?"

Head, face sullen, hesitated and then said, "No sir."

"What objection do you have to propounding your theory, Mr. Head?"

"I realize," Head replied, "that in the eyes of the Commissioner and of the audience I am laughing-stock enough already. I do not propose to make myself more so."

"Very well then, Mr. Hardy . . ."

"However, Mr. Commissioner . . ." Head was on his feet.

It was five minutes of twelve.

"Just a second, Mr. Hardy," the Commissioner said.

"Mr. Commissioner," Head said, his face hopeful once

more. "I do have one request to make. And depending on its outcome, perhaps I shall propound my theory after all. I should like to have Mr. Hardy examined by a physician."

The audience hummed and then broke into laughter.

"You would what?" the Commissioner said.

"I have a very good reason for making that request," Head said. "It has to do with certain physical characteristics . . ."

The Commissioner shrugged. "Is there a doctor in the audience?" he said.

Four rose, and the Commissioner smiled and said, "It is pleasing to see that so many of the medical profession have an interest in our national pastime. . . . Now, Mr. Hardy, I have no idea what Mr. Head is driving at by this unseemly request, but do you have any objection? Are you willing to submit to the examination?"

Joe stared into the audience, his heart pounding. Bess was smiling at him. It was four minutes of twelve.

"Mr. Commissioner," Applegate called, "I object. It would be too time-consuming. Such an examination requires equipment."

"Obviously it could be only a cursory examination," the Commissioner said.

"Cursory's all right with me," Head said.

"Mr. Hardy?" the Commissioner said.

"May I consult with Mr. Applegate a second, sir?"

"Mr. Hardy," the Commissioner said, "do you have misgivings about such an examination?"

"None whatsoever, I'd just like to talk to him."

"Very well."

Joe left the stand.

"It's a tough decision to make, lad," Applegate muttered. "But it has to be your decision, not mine. It's three minutes of twelve. As for me, I'm ready to do whatever you say. I'll abide by the contract."

It has been said, Joe knew, that men near death review their lives in a matter of seconds. His knuckles were white as he grasped the edge of the table.

"But it's going to take at least ten minutes to go through all this physical-examination stuff, that's certain," Applegate said.

"Can you give me an extension?"

"Sorry, Joe. I really can't. A contract's a contract, lad. Although, as I say, I'm ready right now to leave and switch you back, if you say so. But there's not much time."

"That guy Head . . . Where'd he ever get an idea like that?"

"Maybe he wants to see if you have a tail," Applegate said solemnly.

"Mr. Hardy, have you made your decision?" the Commissioner called. "I'd like to get this hearing over with some time before the baseball season ends."

"Of course I could switch you back and then you could take the examination," Applegate said, "but then you'd certainly differ in quite a few respects from Joe Hardy when they looked at you."

Or he could flee. Now. And that would be admitting guilt. He had gotten himself into this mess, and dragged the team in with him. He could desert them now. But for the rest of his life he would have to live with his own cowardice, his own selfishness. And if he did the right thing by the team it meant he would lose his chance; forevermore he would be damned to Applegate. His head began to swim and he felt the room begin to reel. And there was only one thought he could cling to, and this had something to do with: *If I make this sacrifice, it is a good thing to do, and therefore I should be saved from Applegate. But if I take the selfish course and run out, I deserve to be doomed forever.*

But the realities were just the opposite.

"Mr. Hardy . . ."

Joe took a deep breath, looked once at Bess, and then at the Commissioner.

"All right, sir. I'm ready for the examination."

Ten minutes later, Joe and the four doctors stood before the Commissioner.

"Have you gentlemen completed your findings?" the Commissioner said.

"Yes sir," one of the four said. "We find Mr. Hardy completely normal in all respects."

A great cheer rang through the hearing room, and the Commissioner banged his gavel angrily.

"The hearing is still in progress," he shouted. "Mr. Head," he went on menacingly, "would you step up here, please."

Head slunk toward the dais.

"Now Mr. Head, it should seem clear even to you by

now that you have wasted the time of the hearing body, and that furthermore you have cast a completely unwarranted slur on the name of a lad who has been a credit to baseball. You have made yourself appear ridiculous. You have cost the league time and money. All this we know. What I should now like to know, Mr. Head, is on what conceivable evidence you instigated this charge? On what possible flight of fancy did you ever undertake it in the first place?"

"I'm very sorry, sir," Head said weakly. "I only did it for the good of baseball."

"And by no means for the good of the New York Yankees," Applegate said with heavy sarcasm. "I'm telling you, Mr. Commissioner, he's the most frantic Yankee-lover I've ever seen."

Dropping his voice, Applegate said to Joe, "How do you feel, lad?"

Numb was how he felt, but he made no reply. Picking up a pencil, he began to draw circles on a pad of paper.

"That was a courageous thing you did, lad," Applegate said. "I admire your guts and I'll tell you this right now. You won't regret it."

Joe sighed, then glanced up sharply, arrested by what Head was saying.

"I was sitting at my desk one day, sir," Head said, raising his eyes in appeal, "when I got a telephone call from somebody who wouldn't give me his name. They told me Joe Hardy was a big phony and that to prove it all I had to do

was ask a few questions around Hannibal, Missouri. . . .
That's how it started."

"And who was this informant?" the Commissioner said.

"I have no idea, sir, because he wouldn't give his name. I
remember he had a very hoarse, deep voice, and he kept
calling me 'lad.'"

Joe looked quickly at Applegate, who examined his nails
intently, then looked toward the ceiling.

Suddenly, fifteen minutes too late, Joe knew. It had been
Applegate all the way.

And Applegate was saying, "Mr. Commissioner, I ask for
the decision of the hearing body."

"Yes, Mr. Applegate," the Commissioner said, "I think
it is high time for a ruling." Striking the gavel twice, he
stood and said, "the hearing body finds unanimously that
Joe Hardy is—*innocent*. He may rejoin the team tomorrow."

And Joe was surrounded then by the audience, milling
and shoving and cheering, all trying to reach his hand.
And Mr. van Buren was pounding his back, Mr. van Buren
the happiest man in the room unless it was Applegate, and
a second later Joe was aloft on the shoulders of four strong
men, fans all, and nobody seemed to notice his face because
they were all too busy cheering. And Applegate was making a speech.

"Mr. Commissioner, the defense wishes to assure Mr.
Head that although his movements have been ill-con-
sidered throughout, we of the defense hold for him no

grudge, no ill-feeling. Because Mr. Head was motivated, as are we all, by the desire to keep the game of baseball what it has ever been and must ever remain—the cleanest game in the land."

Hearing the insidious tone, struck by the diabolical glint of Applegate's eyes, Joe, from his position high in the air, felt sudden fear and breaking free from the crowd, he fled. Out the door, down the corridor, bypassing the elevator, seeking the stairway, down one flight, and then down another, with no clear idea but to escape.

Flight after flight he descended until there, waiting at the next landing, was Applegate. Smiling.

"Where are you going in such a hurry, lad?" he said.

For a moment, Joe just stared. Then he walked slowly down the three remaining steps. Energy seemed to gather from all over his body, rushed for his right shoulder, coursed down his arm and into his fist, and with all his might he swung for Applegate's jaw.

Afterward he realized that Applegate had not even sidestepped. But the blow had missed, and with its force Joe fell to the floor, fell in a heap on the rich carpet, and before his eyes were the polished tips of Applegate's black and white sport shoes.

"Now don't dash off, lad," Applegate said. "We've got business."

| 22 | It was after three o'clock and they were sitting in a rear booth, he and Applegate, in an all-night eating place. Applegate was hunched low over a mound of chopped chicken livers; Joe was slumped against the wall, on his plate a half-eaten cheeseburger. The lights were low, the juke box turned down, and the room hummed softly with the talk of taxi drivers and others, discussing the next day's entries at Atlantic City.

Joe gazed miserably at Applegate's face, noted its utter lack of concern, its complete absorption in the food he was shoveling in with such élan. Dabbing his mouth with his napkin, Applegate looked up, smiled faintly. "Don't take it so hard, Joe," he said. "Everything's going to be all right. You'll see." Again he applied himself to the chicken livers, and with his mouth full said, "Maybe if I tell you about Roscoe Ent it'll cheer you up a little. Would you like to hear?"

"No," Joe said.

"No what?"

Joe gritted his teeth. "No, sir," he muttered.

Applegate smiled, relenting. "I'm not really going to insist on that, Joe," he said. "As time goes by and you feel you'd like to call me sir voluntarily, then I think it would be a very nice gesture on your part. But I've always thought it was far better to command respect than demand it."

"You're really a crumb, Applegate."

Applegate chuckled.

"You engineered it all, right down to the last lousy detail," Joe said. "You called up Head about Hannibal. You—"

"I'll confess it was all rather clever," Applegate said. "I must also confess that it's been a highly entertaining summer. Oh, not that I haven't been just as clever at other times, but never against such an interesting milieu . . . baseball, I mean . . ."

"You're a crumb," Joe repeated.

Applegate set down his fork abruptly and his tone changed. "Tonight you call me a crumb, Joe. Tonight I tolerate it. But I won't for long, do you understand? Do you?"

"Yeah."

"Yeah what?"

"Just yeah, that's all."

Applegate chuckled. "It's a good thing I'm feeling mellow tonight. . . . Joe, I want to talk briefly with you about your future and I've also got some very interesting pictures to show you, but first I want to tell you about Ent. It's vain of me, I suppose, but . . ."

"You hooked him after all, I see," Joe said.

"No, as a matter of fact I haven't," Applegate said. "Not that I didn't try. Incidentally, Joe, do you feel any different?"

"No."

"Well, you won't for a while. It's gradual. By the way, I won't be able to have the formal indoctrination ceremony for a while yet."

"The what?"

"We always have an indoctrination ceremony," Applegate said, cleansing his plate with the fragment of a roll. "But too many of the fellows are away on vacation right now. I thought in a couple of weeks or so, after they get back . . ."

"I'd be delighted," Joe said grimly.

"Some very nice guys," Applegate said. "You'll be surprised when you see who some of them are. Well, anyway, about Ent. . . . It seems he went into the sausage factory after all. You know . . . fate . . . foreordained pattern and so forth. For years he tried to buck it, first with burlesque, then with baseball, and the night clubs and so on. But after his act flopped that night in Baltimore, he went back home and reported for work at the factory the very next morning."

"Come on, Applegate."

"I'm dead serious. He says he realizes it's what he was always meant to do and he seems very happy, especially since he got married."

"Don't give me all this stuff, Applegate."

"Sure he's married. Three days ago he got married, to that little lady he came with tonight. She's a night-club stripper. You see, Roscoe pretty much came to terms with himself. He realized that all these years of saying he liked burlesque houses and night clubs for the sake of the atmosphere was nothing but pure rationalization. The real reason he liked them was because of the strippers, and I think he's always wanted to have one for his wife. Roscoe's matured quite a bit. He faces things."

"How'd he ever get one to marry him?"

"Well . . ." Applegate snickered.

"You said you didn't . . ."

"I didn't. I tried, but he still wouldn't go for it. However, he was willing to make a separate deal. He was willing to do me a favor in return for the love of this girl we saw tonight and so . . . yes, Joe, you might say I got to the witness . . . Now, take a look at this."

From a manila envelope, he produced a photograph and handed it across the table. "Oh, waitress," he said, "could I have some more of the same please? It was the chicken livers."

The photograph showed a young man skiing, bent forward, bronzed face sharp against a frosty sky. Without even a sense of shock, Joe recognized the face as his own.

"That'll be this winter in the French Alps," Applegate said. "You like?"

Joe tossed the picture aside. "Swell," he said.

"Oh, come on now, Joe, don't be like that. Now here's another one."

The second photograph showed himself and Lola standing before a neat stone cottage. Joe was wearing a beret.

"And that, of course, is you and Lola in Provence this autumn," Applegate said. "That's the house you'll have. Oh, by the way, did I ever tell you about Lola?"

"What about her?"

"Well, quite a while ago, I kind of half-promised you to her after the twenty-first."

"Yes, I've already heard."

"I think you'll find her very companionable," Applegate said. "Do you have any objections? Because if you do, I'm sure I could dig up somebody else equally attractive. The reason I picked out Lola was because she seems your type somehow. She's rather a soft-hearted girl. Too soft-hearted, really. I've had quite a bit of trouble with her in the past, but she's getting better. It all takes time."

His chicken livers arrived, and Applegate moved his fork to the attack. His mouth full again, he said, "The main thing you've got to watch out for, Joe, is conscience. Now unfortunately you've got a very annoying conscience. . . . I never suspected it, really. I had you and your wife figured for a real solid case of incompatibility. . . . Oh, well, it all takes time . . . you'll be okay after a while."

Joe was still studying the picture. "Is all this necessary?" he said.

"Oh, necessary isn't exactly the word," Applegate said. "Let's say it's inevitable. I mean, you see the photographs right there before your eyes, don't you. Now don't go asking philosophical questions, lad. You just get yourself on that boat with Lola and go on over to France and have yourself a time."

"And what if I don't want to go?"

"It's the *Caronia*, I think. Oh, come on, Joe, that's the same thing as asking what if the sun doesn't rise."

"What's this one?" Joe said, picking up another photograph. It showed the interior of a room with a low ceiling. He and Lola were seated on a couch.

"Oh, yeah, the indoor shot," Applegate said. "Didn't turn out bad at all, did it? Yes, that's you and Lola on the night she puts in her claim for you. That's her apartment. That's only a few nights away from now, if I'm not mistaken. It's going to be a night of die-casting, so to speak. After that night's over, boy, you won't even *think* about Joe Boyd again."

Applegate fell silent while he stuffed his mouth. Then he said, "Like I told you, boy, it's all a matter of conscience. Conscience is the root of all inconvenience. Now here's a suggestion. If you find it tough at first, you might try saying, 'I shall have no conscience whatsoever' or something like that, twenty or thirty times a day. Some of our people have found that helpful."

"What's this one?" Joe asked.

"Hey, wait a minute," Applegate said agitatedly. He grabbed for the photograph. "That's not supposed to be in there."

But Joe moved it beyond Applegate's reach, and the anger swiftly mounted as he realized the photograph's meaning.

It showed him wearing the uniform of the New York Yankees.

"What's the lousy idea, Applegate?" he said, and for the second time that night he had the overwhelming impulse to swing at Applegate's jaw, but this time restrained it.

"I didn't mean for you to see that," Applegate said, "but as long as you've seen it there's nothing I can do about it. You shouldn't be so grabby."

"This had better not mean what I think it means, buster, that's all I can say," Joe said, looking Applegate full in the eye.

"I'm afraid that's precisely what it means, Joe," Applegate said cheerfully. "During the winter you'll be traded to the Yankees."

"That's what you think, you lousy crumb," Joe said and deliberately he tore the photograph into pieces.

"Oh, come now, Joe, be a sport. Don't be petty. Do you think tearing it up is going to change anything? That's childish. Look at it this way. You're just too good a ball player not to be playing for the Yankees, that's all. So you'll be traded."

Joe did not reply. His eye had been caught by a fragment of caption. Quickly he put the pieces together again. And he saw now that the caption read, "Joe Hardy, of the World's Champion New York Yankees."

"World's Champion New York Yankees!" he exploded. "How are the Yankees gonna be any world's champions? The Senators are going to win the pennant."

Applegate smiled apologetically, looking down at his plate. "Joe, I guess I might as well tell you the worst and get it over with. The Senators aren't going to win the pennant at all."

Refusing now to meet Joe's eye, Applegate went on, "You see, Joe, Old Man Welch was right without knowing it. Because my first allegiance really is to the Yankees." He looked up and his eyes now gleamed like steel. "Joe, I've been a Yankee fan for years and I couldn't let them down. I just wanted to have some fun. You see the point, don't you?"

"This is the lousiest of all," Joe said in a quiet measured voice. "I really hate your guts, Applegate."

"Well, now, as far as that goes, lad, you can't say I broke the contract . . ."

"Shut up."

"I said I'd make you a great player and I have. And you're still a great player. You'll always be a great player as long as you behave yourself. It's just . . . as I say . . . my first allegiance is to the Yankees . . ."

"You dirty, lousy . . ."

"Now, what's going to happen is this," Applegate went on, unruffled. "We might as well give the fans their money's worth. You guys are going to pick up whatever ground you still need, and going into the last day of the season you and the Yankees will be tied. Clever, eh? Now wait a minute . . ."

Applegate drew a card from his inside coat pocket. "Now according to the schedule," he said, "you guys play the Yankees that day. Well, that'll be a climactic game, all right. It sure will be a climactic game. It ought to be something to see."

Joe rose abruptly. "Yeah, come out and see it, Applegate. Listen, do me a favor," he said nastily. "If I throw that ketchup bottle will you hold your head still?"

Applegate shook his head, smiling.

"What's the matter, you yellow?" Turning, Joe strode angrily for the front door, shouting over his shoulder, "Come out and see it, buster, and you'll see the Yankees get their noses rubbed in the dirt."

But as he swung open the door and walked out into the stillness of four o'clock in the morning, he knew that his words were empty, knew that back in the booth Applegate was chuckling over his chicken livers.

	"Joe, darling, I'm so sorry you can't be a little
23	happier about it," Lola said. "But what am I
	to do? Mr. Applegate said it would be okay,
	and I've been waiting *so* long."

It was a week later, the eve of the final game of the season, and he and Lola were sitting on the sofa in the living room of her apartment, a low-ceilinged room with white walls. On Joe's right hung a huge oil painting, a softer-textured replica of the photograph of himself and Lola standing before the little house in Provence.

"It's not your fault, Lola," he said, staring gloomily at the beret. "And as far as that goes, if it has to be somebody, I'd far rather it would be you."

She took his hand. "I'm glad to know that, anyway, Joe. In other words it's not me you find unattractive but the principle of the thing."

He nodded miserably.

"I understand," she said. "You poor darling."

Sympathetically she began patting his hand, but he could not help noticing an expression akin to cupidity cross her face as she glanced up toward the gray door with the glass knob; the gray door at which Joe himself had been staring uneasily ever since his arrival.

"Well, don't worry about it for a while," she said, still

caressing his hand. "The evening's young yet, and you're probably still a little tired from the game this afternoon. Now let's just relax."

She slid lower on the couch and he glanced at her, then looked quickly away, feeling the old disquietude. For the occasion she wore a tight-fitting bodice of semi-low cut, and over it a bolero jacket, all in maroon linen. And it was remarkable in one way, although quite unremarkable in another, Joe thought, that all through the summer it had been only Lola who had the power to make him waver. Never Applegate. Never the team. Just Lola. And it was also true, or at least so he told himself, that it was not really her beauty that created this power but her essential goodness as a person.

"Tell me about the team, Joe," she said softly.

Joe grunted.

"On second thought, don't," she said. "I don't want to hear about the team. It must be simply heartbreaking."

"It's a terrible thing to watch," Joe said.

"I think letting them catch up with the Yankees is one of the meanest things Applegate has ever done," she said, "and furthermore I'm going to tell him so."

Joe nodded unhappily.

"Poor team," she said.

Poor team. With heavy heart he had played out these final days of the season, knowing bitter pain at every turn: pain to glance up and catch the expression of hope on the seamed face of old Mr. Welch; pain to hear Mr. van Buren say happily, "Boy, am I glad *you* got acquitted!"; pain to see the mounting excitement and hope of the team, and of the fans; pain to know that it was being called now a team of destiny. He alone knew how cruel the destiny. And in a large sense he was only making it the more cruel when he continued to hit home runs, by moving the team nearer and nearer to a prize that could not be theirs. And yet he could not stop, not even this afternoon when he had hit two home runs to clinch the game that moved the Senators into a tie, but a tie that would be broken so sadistically in tomorrow's finale.

"Joe," Lola said. "Do you want to know something foolish?"

"What?"

"I'm already packed. Even though we don't leave for another ten days, I'm all ready to sail. Isn't that childish?"

When he did not reply, she said, "Oh, darling, it really *is* going to be such fun. Provence is such a gorgeous place. I know that once you get there you'll love it. You see, it really is true what Applegate says about conscience. You just have to try real hard. We'll both try real hard. I really shouldn't be talking so big because I'm not completely cured yet, not by any means . . . Listen, darling, I still think you'd feel better if you'd let me fix you a drink."

"No, thanks."

"Not even a little one? It would help relax you."

He followed her glance toward the gray door.

"No, thanks," he said.

She sighed. "I've tried, Joe. You can't say I haven't tried to make it easy for you."

"I know. I said I wasn't blaming you."

"You see, darling," she went on, "I really can't blame myself too much. And I can't feel too guilty. For this reason. If Applegate hadn't assigned you to me he might have given you a far worse assignment."

"I realize that," Joe said. He sighed heavily. "Let me think for a while."

"Take as long as you like, Joe," she said, looking again toward the gray door.

A half hour passed in silence. Joe slumped lower and gradually lower on the couch, at times closing his eyes, then opening them, to be confronted with the slimness of Lola's ankle and, beyond, the gray door. From somewhere in another part of the house there was the sound of hammering, someone perhaps hanging a picture. For Lola's quarters were not an apartment in the ordinary sense. They were two rooms, living room and bedroom, on the third floor of an old house, in a neighborhood remarkable for its aura of antiquity.

When he opened his eyes again, she was looking full at him, and he noticed again how soft were her lashes, how devastatingly beautiful her face. He reached out a hand, moved it slowly up the back of her neck. Then he rose and walked over to the gray door and turned.

"Okay, Lola," he said.

She did not rise. She merely continued to look at him from the beautiful eyes.

"Okay?" he said.

"Come here, Joe," she said. "Come sit down again for a second."

Slowly he recrossed the room. "What's wrong?"

"Sit down, darling."

For perhaps a full minute she gazed pensively at the oil painting, at times seeming about to smile, at others to cry.

"Lola, what is it?" he asked finally.

"You're a wonderful guy, Joe," she said, "But I can't make you do it. Something inside just won't let me. While you had your eyes closed, I was watching your face, and for the first time it came to me how truly miserable you are. You are miserable, aren't you, Joe?"

He nodded, looking at the floor. "But I don't want you to think it's because I don't like you," he said.

"I realize that, darling, and it makes me glad. But I simply can't make you do it. Mr. Applegate or no Mr. Applegate. The only thing I ask is that you leave, right now. The longer you stay, the more painful it is for me . . ."

She bit her lip and her eyes filled with tears.

"I'm sorry, Lola," he said, rising, touching her head.

"Don't touch me, Joe, please. That only makes it worse." Her voice breaking now, she said, "I only wish you didn't exist any more. I wish you had won instead of Mr. Applegate. I wish Mr. Applegate had never picked you in the first place. He usually has better judgment. I wish you had stopped being Joe Hardy on September twenty-first . . ."

Burying her face on the arm of the sofa, she began weeping uncontrollably.

"That's what I want more than anything else in the world, Lola," he said gently. "Can you help me stop being Joe Hardy?"

"It's impossible now," she said, her voice muffled. "And even if it were possible, it would mean such a horrible punishment for me that I couldn't begin to describe it." Again the racking sobs began.

"All right, Lola," he said. "I'll be going now. And thanks."

"Yes, please, Joe. Please go now."

And rising, she ran swiftly across to the gray door and yanked it open. He caught a glimpse of her tear-stained face, and then she was flopping face down on her bed.

"I'll see you later, Lola," he said.

And the thing about all this, he thought, as he walked down the narrow staircase, is that nothing ever gets better. Always and always worse.

At the foot of the stairway was the side entrance by which he had arrived. A little bell tinkled as he opened the door and stepped out into a small bricked courtyard. There was a wishing well he had noticed on the way in. He walked to it, feeling in his pocket for a coin. For a moment he stood there, hand still in pocket, then turned slowly away. It was beyond wishing. All that remained was bravery; or perhaps stoicism was the better word.

24 September 29, 1958, was a bright crisp day in the nation's capital. The wind had shifted during the night, and all over the city the flags were standing out to the southeast against a deep blue sky.

The flags were what Joe noticed first that morning when he rose and looked from the window of his hotel room. The flags: and then the taste of the autumnal air, a taste to stir the memory. For years it had been such weather as this that he had awaited through the long, humid Washington summers. In the past on such a day he would have stepped whistling from the house, grateful that the worst had finally ended, happy in his job.

It was ironic that such weather had been chosen for what surely would be the most miserable day of his life. Miserable not alone for his own sake, but for the misery he knew would come to an entire city; to an entire country, or surely that part of it lying west of the Hudson River.

Standing by the window, looking down at the street, seeing the people stream forth from the trolleys, walk briskly to their jobs, he winced with guilt. On the lips of these people, and those like them all over the city, there could be no conceivable topic but the game; in their hearts nothing less than confidence of victory. For why else would a team be lifted from the abyss and led so far if not intended for victory? Anything less would be cruelly incomprehensible. And it was he, Joe Hardy, the greedy and the gullible, who had led them within sight of the vision and who must stand helplessly by now while the vision was snatched away.

Team of destiny . . .

"Joe," said his waitress at breakfast, "I got ten dollars bet on you with my cousin in The Bronx, and I'm already counting the money."

Looking up from his eggs, he smiled, unable to reply.

After breakfast, he walked, and on every side he could feel the drama. It spoke from the newspaper headlines, from the makeshift scoreboards erected in shop windows; from the television sets assigned this day to the use of sidewalk viewers; and it spoke from the faces of the people themselves, from their greetings and snatches of conversation.

"It's Ransom gonna pitch."

"Ransom's only had two days' rest."

"It's still gonna be Ransom. That's what van Buren said."

There is a quality in the human soul, perverseness perhaps, that keeps hoping even when the cards are stacked, even when there is no hope. And for fleeting moments, feeling the drama, the excitement, Joe forgot Applegate;

for fleeting moments he let himself feel the hope these people were feeling.

At other times, as he walked the familiar blocks near the hotel, blocks now transformed by the holiday atmosphere, he told himself that at least he had been able to give them this much. Today they were part of a setting, part of a drama, which all the world watched. He had given them pride of team; he had given them admiration for the fantastic feat the team had accomplished since July. He had given them . . .

But these thoughts gave him no comfort. They were specious, just as hope was self-torture.

He was dressing for the game, surrounded by guys alive with excitement, guys exchanging determined promises, guys with whom he would not be playing after today. After today . . .

Hearing them was pain. And there was pain in watching Benny van Buren's attempt to maintain a crusty, taciturn, managerial air, when it was apparent that inside he was fluttering. For Mr. van Buren, like the fans, could not believe that a team so singled out by destiny could be left hanging in second place.

Now Mr. van Buren was opening a telegram, tacking it with others on the dressing-room bulletin board. Telegrams from well-wishers all over the globe, one from a fan in the Fiji Islands.

Mr. van Buren cleared his throat to speak. Standing near him was Mr. Welch, bundled now in his heavy winter overcoat since the change in weather, his eyes shining.

"Fellows," Mr. van Buren was saying, "first of all I wanna announce that it'll be Ransom going for us today, and we couldn't put the ball in better hands . . ."

Sammy Ransom. Sammy of the gaunt, impassive visage . . . Sammy who would be pitching with only two days' rest . . . who, in the late innings, would lose the snap from his fireball and then would try to get by on heart alone . . . Sammy who had no way of knowing that heart stood for nothing with a slob named Applegate.

"And I also wanna say this," Mr. van Buren continued. "I hope we win today. I'm expecting to win. But whether we win or lose, I want to tell you guys that you've given me joy that seldom comes to a manager. You guys have played the greatest baseball I've ever seen in my life . . ."

And when Mr. van Buren concluded, up jumped Rocky Pratt, a regenerated character by now, a man of team spirit, a man who never complained of headaches from excessive TV viewing. "Listen, Ben," he shouted, "all that stuff sounds fine, but there's just one thing wrong with it. We're not gonna lose. We're gonna win. Hey, you guys, who's thinking about losing?"

"Nobody," was the answering chorus.

"Then let's go out there and *win*," Pratt thundered.

An ovation rocked the park as the team took the field. It was a park this day jammed to the aisles. Even to its far reaches, there was not an empty seat . . . except . . .

Trotting out to his right-field post, Joe looked, and after

the National Anthem was played, looked again. Two empty seats there were. Neither Applegate nor Lola was in the seat to which their season tickets entitled them. Applegate, so confident of the outcome that he disdained even to be a witness. And Lola . . . perhaps absent from heartbreak. But who could say about Lola?

The plate umpire signaled to play ball. Ransom peered in for his signal, wound up, let fire, and thus began a game that would live forever in the minds of men.

Pitching for the Yankees that day was Bix Kilgallen, a right-hander who already had twenty-three victories to his credit, and who, like Ransom, was a fireballer. But Kilgallen was not right that day; if Applegate was determined to exact the quintessence in cruelty, he could not be managing it more expertly, Joe thought. Even to the last he was dangling the bait.

For after the Yankees went out in order in the first, Joe came up in the Senators' half and rifled the second pitch on a line to deepest center. With his great speed, he beat the relay for an inside-the-park home run, and the score was one to nothing. The ball park rocked with sound. The Yankees, although they still conducted themselves with the mien of champions, now looked not so tall in their uniforms, nor so lethal at bat.

And in the fourth, Joe, up again, lashed a towering drive over the scoreboard in right center. Although Joe's two homers were the only hits Kilgallen had yielded, he was yanked then in favor of Buttons Avery, the Yankees' venerable relief artist, famed for his control and his poise in the clutch.

Meanwhile Ransom, his fast ball kicking like a live thing, was mowing down the champions with the precision of a machine-gunner. A single to left in the second, a scratch hit in the fifth, were all the Yankees could muster. In the sixth, his control momentarily gone, he walked the first two batters but steadied and came out of the frame unscathed.

And Joe, first man up in the seventh, doubled sharply to right center. A bunt and a long fly brought him around, and the score was three to nothing.

Although the ball park was still rocking, it was with sadness that Joe returned to the bench and sat watching while Sammy Ransom stroked the rabbit's foot Rocky Pratt had supplied for the occasion, the rabbit's foot he had been stroking between innings all through the game. How pitiably impotent was a rabbit's foot compared with what the Yankees had going for them today.

And yet, where was Applegate?

As Joe took the field for the eighth, it occurred to him there was nothing to prevent Applegate from occupying a seat in some other part of the stadium. A ruse of that sort would be completely in character, and he scanned the upper decks, looking for a flash of bright yellow sports shirt. There were these in plenty but no wearer, at least at such a distance, did he recognize as Applegate.

Nor did Applegate appear in the Senators' half of the eighth.

The ninth began, and although it was against his better judgment, Joe dared to hope.

The stands were hushed now, as tensely silent as they had been that day in Philadelphia before he had spoiled poor Bobby Schantz's no-hitter.

Only three outs away. Joe leaned forward as Ransom faced the first Yankee batter; Ransom, who had performed so gallantly. Three quick outs . . .

"Joe Hardy stinks out loud."

The rasping voice left no doubt. There sat Applegate in his accustomed seat.

"You stink, Hardy," he shouted.

Applegate, on his feet, brandishing a rolled score card, and holding his nose.

And then Joe could look no more because the first Yankee lined a ball over his head which he turned and chased to the base of the right-field wall, taking the carom neatly and whipping it into the infield in time to hold the hit to a double.

Applegate was fluttering his handkerchief in Joe's direction.

And Joe knew this was it.

The next batter singled sharply to center. The run scored, and it was now three to one.

"How d'ya like that, Hardy?" Applegate was shouting. The partisan crowd was telling him to shut up and sit down but he took no notice. "That's the first one, Hardy," he bellowed. "And you ain't seen nothing yet."

And it was true. In quick succession, the next two Yankee batters pumped singles to left and center, scoring another run and putting men on first and third. It was now three to two, and the gallant Ransom had had it. With slumped shoulders, he stood near the mound while a relief pitcher was called in from the bullpen.

"You lousy four-flusher, Hardy," Applegate was yelling.

The relief man was Bill Gregson, who had saved many a game for the team that summer. Van Buren could have made no better choice. Working craftily, Gregson got the first batter he faced on a long fly to left. That was out number one, but it also scored the runner from third, and the score now was tied at three to three, with a man still on first. Shaving the corners too closely, Gregson walked the next man, but the one following went out on a pop-up behind second.

"Okay, Hardy," Applegate yelled. "This is it right here. This is the ball game, old pal."

Not doubting it, Joe leaned forward. The runners led off. Gregson wound up, delivered. Ball one. Then strike one, and then . . .

The hit was a humpback, arching softly over the second baseman's head toward short right field and sinking fast. The Yankee runners were streaking down the base paths. And Joe Hardy was digging straight ahead, digging for the last notch of speed, diving with outstretched glove, and picking the ball off the grass tops, then falling hard to the ground, rolling over and over, but with his bare hand holding the ball aloft to prove it had been caught, and the roar that surged through the park was as much a roar of amazement as applause.

Picking himself up, Joe glanced at Applegate, who sat glumly back in his seat, and Joe realized that not even Applegate had expected him to catch that ball, realized it had been meant to fall safely, and that other hits would have followed, breaking the game wide open in favor of the Yankees, putting it beyond reach, and giving the Yankees their tenth consecutive pennant.

And as he trotted back to the bench, doffing his cap to the roar of the crowd, he realized something else. There was an acute pain in his right shoulder where he had hit the ground. And he felt suddenly winded, very tired. He, who had felt neither physical pain nor fatigue since the night of July twenty-first.

All's fair in love and war, Applegate had said. Applegate had not expected him to make that catch. Applegate was capable of playing it as dirty as the occasion demanded . . .

He felt his stomach. It was still flat and hard.

The bench was silent, except for Mr. van Buren, who kept muttering over and over, as a man in a trance, "You saved it for us, Joe. That catch saved it for us. Can you win it for us now, Joe?"

Third up, Joe walked slowly over and selected a bat, then stooped at the edge of the dugout and watched while the first batter flied out to left.

One away. He advanced to the on-deck circle. *No, Ben,*

I don't think I can do it this time. He looked up at the clear, blue sky beyond the left-field grandstand. *I've done it for you all season, but not this time. There's a guy sitting out there along the right-field line. I'm afraid he's too much for us, Ben.*

Two away.

Joe strode to the plate, and the sound that rose on the afternoon air was an appeal, a concerted plea from thirty thousand fans, who seemed to sense that if the Senators didn't win it here and now with Hardy, the Yankees would wrap it up in the tenth, and second place would be a bitter reality.

Joe stepped in, set his spikes. *Even if I can't hit the one we need,* he thought, *it would be the greatest pleasure in the world to hit a hard one foul into the right-field boxes, maybe catch Applegate off guard.*

But that was trivial now.

He faced the pitcher.

The ball zipped in. Joe didn't offer. He was reminded of that first day in Detroit when he had faced Rocky Pratt. He had frozen then, and the feeling was the same now.

Strike two, and again he hadn't offered.

You've got no guts. And Applegate wins everything. He's made a monkey of you at every turn.

But his shoulder ached, and he felt very tired.

The Yankee pitcher curved one wide of the plate, tempting him. And it was now strike two, ball one.

The windup, and it was coming in, letter-high, near the outside corner, and with all his strength Joe swung, saw

· 231 ·

the ball start out on a line toward deep center field; and he was streaking for first, saw the ball clear the center fielder's head; and he was moving for second and the ball was rolling all the way to the center-field wall, the center fielder in pursuit; and he was digging for third and ahead of him he saw the third-base coach, flailing his arms, signaling him to go all the way.

And when it happened it was like a medicine ball, hard in the stomach. Joe faltered; then, clenching his fists, came on again, rounded third and headed for home, but now his temples pounded and his stomach quivered out ahead of him and his breath was coming in short, dry, harsh sobs, and the uniform was too tight, and his legs felt like wood. But he lumbered on down the third-base line, a third-base line that seemed unfamiliar now, and the figure of the Yankee catcher was like a giant in armor, standing there, blocking the plate. And Joe slid, reaching with his toe for a corner of the plate. And the ground came up hard to meet him, jolting his whole body. And the ball was jabbed hard against his thigh, like a hammer blow. He heard the umpire yell "safe!" and then he was rolling over and over, away from the plate, reaching for his cap, jamming it tight over his head, keeping his face to the ground, because he knew now that he was a middle-aged real-estate salesman named Joe Boyd.

He saw the Yankee catcher turn with a bellow of rage to confront the umpire; saw the whole Yankee infield and then the outfield, and then the bench rush for the umpire, bellowing as they came; and then the Senators were rushing up from their own bench. And keeping low to the ground, dodging among the swarming players, and moving at times animal-like on all fours, he reached the now-empty dugout and, still bent low, descended the steps leading to the dressing room. At the bottom he paused, and, mounting one step, peered cautiously over the coping.

The melee was furious. The Yankee catcher angrily dashed his cap to the ground. Yankee players confronted the umpire chest to chest, and then, running in from right field, came Applegate.

Snatching up the catcher's cap from the ground, he jammed it onto his own head and advanced menacingly on the beleaguered plate umpire. Jaw out-thrust, he began to bark insults about the umpire's judgment, eyesight, ancestry, and sense of direction.

The umpire stood firm, arms folded, head held high, face inscrutable. For a few seconds he endured the tirade, then turned his back, but Applegate circled with him, jaw thrust even closer now, banging fist into palm.

Mr. van Buren stood aside from the fray, smiling, and as Joe watched he was joined by Mr. Welch, also smiling. Mr. Van Buren draped an arm over the old man's shoulder, then bent slightly so that Mr. Welch could do likewise, and they stood, smiling, the manager and the owner of a pennant winner.

For the umpire, with a final nervous flick at the plate with his whiskbroom, was turning and heading off the field, still nagged by Applegate and the Yankees, but still imperiously adamant.

As they advanced, Joe ducked and fled into the dressing room; and although he knew his misery would be compounded now; although he knew he would be subjected to the rigors of hell without even the saving grace of youth and athletic prowess, even so the victory had been won, and he could not resist a glow of triumph. For this moment, at least, what did it matter that his personal punishment would be fearsome? Applegate, for once, had been foiled. The Senators had copped the pennant. The Yankees were finally a second-place team.

Nor could he resist a faint smile at the memory of Applegate's enraged countenance as he confronted the umpire. For the afternoon had proved an axiom long known to baseball men, and known now even to Applegate.

And this was that not even the devil could force an umpire to change his decision.

But his moment of elation was brief.

25 With no clear idea of what he would do, or where he would go, hoping for the sake of the team to hide his own identity, he grabbed an old raincoat from another player's locker and ran out under the grandstand, relieved at least that his nakedness was now covered, for although it was a baseball uniform it seemed now like nakedness. But there was still nothing to silence the clatter of his spiked shoes.

Vaguely thinking that he would find a taxi, and already resolving to take without whimpering whatever punishment Applegate might inflict, he headed out from the park and had gone two blocks when he saw her, running in his direction, carrying a small overnight bag.

"Lola!"

She stopped short, then came ahead, looking at him with bewilderment. "Joe," she said as she reached him. "Poor Joe." She was wearing a black suit, severe in cut. "This is the way you are?"

Crestfallen, he nodded, turning up the lapels of the raincoat, brushing at a wisp of gray hair that fluttered in the wind.

"Joe, did the team win?"

"Yes, they won."

"Oh, even your voice is different. You're cute this way. They really won? Oh, I'm so glad. I've been running all the way."

Her dark hair was tousled like a child's. She stood breathing heavily, lips parted. Never had she been so beautiful, never her skin so clear, her voice so warm. And yet, although she smiled, although she said it was nice about the team, there was something frightened about her eyes.

"For once I beat Applegate," Joe said. "Now it's his turn to take it out on me." He patted his stomach ruefully. "In fact he's already started to take it out on me."

Lola shook her head smiling.

"Am I that funny looking?" he said.

"No, you're darling, Joe. . . . Joe, . . . you don't have to worry about Applegate taking anything out on you."

With singing and shouting, the crowd was surging from the ball park now.

"What do you mean?" he asked.

"You don't want anybody to see you with that uniform on, do you, Joe? Let's go down this little alley here."

She led the way, stopping by a telephone pole. It was a blind alley, a short alley, tucked behind a row of stores, and lined with trash cans and boxes. The afternoon sun glinted over broken cobbles.

"What do you mean, Lola?" he repeated.

"I mean you're free, Joe."

For perhaps ten seconds he stared at her, speechless.

She was facing the waning sun, and her eyes sparkled. For these seconds her look was brilliant.

"Free?" he asked finally, incredulously.

"Yes, Joe, free."

"But *how?*"

"There isn't time to tell you now, Joe. Here." She handed him the overnight bag, and he realized guiltily that he hadn't even offered to carry it for her. "I knew you'd need some clothes. I thought you could change in a gasoline station or some place."

"But Lola . . ."

"You'd better leave me now, Joe. Go back to your life. Don't stand here any more. Don't look at me. Because it's going to happen any minute. . . . I really took a risk even coming here."

"What do you mean?" He gazed at her in consternation, caught her hand. "What's going to happen, Lola?"

"No, Joe. Please don't touch me. You'll be sorry. I'm— he's going to switch me back," she cried desperately.

"To what you were before?"

"Yes, Joe, only I won't be free. I'll just be—ugly."

"Lola . . ."

She bit her lip. He looked at her steadfastly, forgetting that he was no longer Joe Hardy, entranced as always by the lovely eyes, the long sweeping lashes, moistening now.

"But why did you do it, Lola?" he said.

"I guess because I loved a guy named Joe Hardy," she said. "Will you go now, Joe?"

But he could not leave her. He could not move. His feet were frozen to the cobblestones.

"But how did you do it, Lola?"

"Is it so important, Joe?"

"No, it really isn't important. I'm sorry."

"I'll tell you, Joe, if you'll face the other direction; if you'll promise not to look back at me. Because I know it's going to happen any second now."

Reluctantly he turned. A crowd was surging past the alley entrance. He set the overnight bag down and stood behind it to hide his shoes.

"Okay, Lola."

"All right, Joe, now please don't turn around. . . . I played a trick on Mr. Applegate. You know how he feels about food . . . what a repulsive glutton he is. I starved him until he promised to set you free. I stole his shoes, his entire stock of shoes, and I hid them."

"Stole his shoes?"

"Applegate has cloven feet, Joe, just like the books say. He's very sensitive about them. They're very ugly. He can't appear in public without his shoes. He has them specially made. So I hid them until he promised to set you free. Only I forgot to insist on any special time. He picked his own time."

Her voice, and Lola now was only a voice, stopped.

When he remained silent, she said, "Did you hear me, Joe. Do you understand?"

"Yes, Lola, I understand." He could say no more for the lump in his throat.

"Did he pick an embarrassing time to do it, Joe?"

"Yes, but I made it . . . has it happened yet, Lola?"

"Not yet."

"Will you tell me one more thing, Lola? Will you tell me what you were like . . . before?"

She sighed deeply. "I was a school teacher, Joe, and I wasn't very pretty. I was fifty years old and I was still an old maid. The only date I ever had in my life was when I was sixteen years old. Then one day Applegate approached me while I had a class of children going through Mount Vernon. You see, it was really true that I always loved Mount Vernon—but we never did get there, did we?"

"No," he said. "No . . . Lola, I feel like I'm going to bust out and cry."

"Don't, Joe. Don't feel bad. Take your freedom. As for me, well—" Her voice broke. "I'll always remember a beautiful young man named Joe Hardy. I'll always remember a beautiful night in a canoe, on a dark river . . ."

"Lola . . ."

"You gave me something better than all the counts and dukes and movie stars that Applegate provided. For the first time in my life I knew what it meant to be in love."

He turned, and she said sharply, "Please don't."

Obediently he turned back, still not believing, for as she had ducked her head aside, he had glimpsed once again the nape of her neck, the soft hair tousled above it, the clean dark line of the suit collar. . . . It was incredible that such beauty could simply be obliterated, simply disappear.

"But Lola," he said, "I don't mind if you see me like this. Why do you mind so much if I see you?"

"I always want you to remember me like this, Joe. Never anything else. It's—my final vanity, I suppose. Will you go now, darling?"

"I'm not sure I should go, Lola," he said. "After all we've been through, after all you've done for me . . ."

"You have a wife to return to, Joe."

"I know, but somehow I feel it's you I should be with. I feel . . . maybe we should settle down . . . a middle-aged couple . . ."

But even as the words left his lips, he knew he could not mean them.

"Don't talk that way, Joe. I know something of how your wife must feel. . . . Joe, if you ever get tired of your wife again, remember . . ."

He heard her gasp, and when she spoke again her voice had a different note; it was the same voice, soft and cultured, but it was no longer the voice of a young woman.

"Now it's happened, Joe . . ."

He sighed. "I don't know what to say now, Lola."

"There's nothing else to say, Joe. Just go . . . darling."

"Good-bye, Lola."

Picking up the bag, he walked slowly down the alley, walked in the path of the sun, toward the sound of the crowd. Behind him he heard her begin to sob, but he did not turn. He faced straight ahead. That was the very least he could do for her.

26

Dressed now in the clothes Lola had provided, he walked through the streets of the city, walked endlessly through the autumnal chill.

It was a city gone wild. The papers were out. Headlines heralded the triumph. There were victory processions, and in the streets there was dancing.

But Joe Boyd could feel no elation. He could be glad for the sake of some; for Mr. van Buren and Mr. Welch; for those who danced and shouted and who, when darkness fell, would circle bonfires.

He paused before a drug store, looking at a stack of newspapers. A late edition. The banner headline now said:

NATS WHIP YANKS, COP FLAG; HARDY MISSING

Of course. He smiled faintly. "Hardy missing." A problem for somebody. But not for him, not for Joe Boyd.

Walking on through the deepening twilight, it was of Lola that he thought; of her sacrifice; of the way her eyes had looked, of her strangled sob as he had walked away down the alley.

When he reckoned it up, his entire relationship with Lola had been one of desertion. He had deserted her in the traffic jam; in the canoe; in her apartment; and now, this afternoon, for good.

He was terribly tired. The pain where the Yankee catcher had jabbed him with the ball—it was no throb of valor, as he had at first imagined; it was just a dull pain in an old man's leg.

Darkness fell, and he was going where? He ought to find Lola, to help her bear her punishment.

But with every step, he was heading always in the direction of home. It was the life he belonged to. It was the only possible life. Ever since July twenty-first, it was the life he had been fighting for.

But he would always remember Lola, remember with pain. He knew there would be times when he would wake in the dead of night, thinking perhaps that he had heard her voice. The voice of a girl who had compounded her own doom so that he could be saved. The voice of a girl who had disappeared forever.

Perhaps the victory, after all, belonged to Applegate.

It was late at night, and Joe had reached his old neighborhood, was entering a familiar block. Right here, on that night long ago, was where Applegate, a figure in black, had stepped forth from the shadows. "Good evening, Mr. Boyd," he had said, and they had walked on, step for step.

Half expectantly, he scanned the block. But there was now no sign of Applegate and, head lowered, he limped on.

"Joe!"

He halted in his tracks, looking.

"Over here, Joe."

Applegate was seated on the coping of a low brick wall. He wore his sports shirt and Panama hat.

"Come on, old friend, have a seat," he said. "You must be tired."

Joe snorted. "Old friend!"

"Sure, what's wrong with that, Joe? Sure I consider you an old friend. After all we went through this summer. Come on, have a seat."

"No thanks. What's on your mind, Applegate?"

"Oh, nothing much," Applegate said casually, and his tone was one Joe had come to recognize as evasive.

"Where's that music coming from?" Joe asked.

"Oh." Applegate reached out along the lawn and patted something. "It's my portable radio. I'm just listening to a little dance music."

"You never carried any portable radio around before."

"Didn't you ever see it before? Well, I've got it tonight. . . . So, you're headed home, eh, Joe?" Applegate's voice contained the hint of a sneer, but he quickly added, "It's your choice, lad. I'm not going to criticize you for it. Every man to his own choice."

"What's on your mind?" Joe repeated, conscious of something ominous about the way Applegate was acting. "What are you gonna do, shoot me?"

"Shoot you, Joe?" Applegate laughed. "I just dropped around to make sure there were no hard feelings. I also wanted you to know that you're the first guy I've lost on a deal like this since 1601. You looked good out there this afternoon, boy. I guess I ought to congratulate you . . . although you wouldn't have beat me if it hadn't been for Lola."

"And you sure took care of that in a hurry, didn't you? You lousy crumb!" Joe said, suddenly enraged. "You let her have it right in the teeth. That was a real brave thing to do."

"Couldn't be helped, lad," Applegate said quietly. "Like I've told you before, when you're running an organization as big as mine, you've got to enforce some discipline."

"That wasn't discipline, Applegate. That was just plain revenge."

"Helps discipline the others," Applegate said. "Makes her an example."

Joe sighed heavily and dropped to a seat on the coping, a good distance from Applegate.

"What makes you such a heel, anyway, Applegate?" he said. "I mean here I've been watching all summer, and in a lot of ways you seem to have some very decent instincts. And yet everything you do is crumby."

Applegate didn't answer immediately. He was picking blades of grass along the edge of the coping.

"I don't really know myself, Joe," he said finally. "But I can tell you this much. It's not an easy life. I guess everybody pictures me rampaging around the world on a constant bender; a real wild, unbridled character, having a wonderful time . . . but it's not that way at all, Joe. You should know that now."

"But why don't you turn over a new leaf or something? What's wrong with you?"

"I honestly don't know, Joe. I had a few sessions with a psychoanalyst a couple of years ago but all he came up with was a few old bromides like power-fixation and early rejection. I knew all that stuff myself." Applegate sighed. "My life is very long and sometimes I get tired."

"Did he know who you were?"

"Oh, sure, he was one of us."

"But you can't just—" Joe began and then stopped, for a voice on Applegate's portable radio had said:

"Ladies and gentlemen, we interrupt this program to bring you a bulletin from the WDDC newsroom," and now another voice was saying:

"A special bulletin. Joe Hardy has been found. We repeat, Joe Hardy has been found. The star right fielder returned to his hotel shortly after ten-thirty this evening. He told reporters that he had merely been out visiting some friends for dinner. Young Hardy was the object of a city-wide search all evening. He turned up missing directly after his game-winning home run this afternoon. But he is now safe and sound. We return you to . . ."

Joe sighed heavily. "Okay, Applegate, let's have it. What are you trying to pull now?"

Applegate snickered and snapped the radio off. "Must be kind of a shock to hear that, isn't it, Joe?"

"Maybe it'll be a shock to you and some other people, the Baseball Commissioner for instance, when I call up and say this Joe Hardy is a fake."

"You wouldn't do that, would you, Joe? Not to an old friend."

"And here's one witness you won't be able to get to. You'll be dealing with Joe Boyd, not Roscoe Ent."

Applegate sat erect. "I had to do it, Joe. Now here's the deal," he said, his voice all business. "I'm here to ask you a favor. I can't make you do it. I'm just relying on your friendship. Cigarette?"

"No."

"Okay. It's this way. Here's the World Series coming up and no Joe Hardy. And who's the team playing against in the World Series? The Dodgers. Okay. And without you in there, the Dodgers are a sure shot to win in four games. Right? Okay. Now I've never told you this but it just happens that I hate the Dodgers even more than I love the Yankees, if you see what I mean. I mean I couldn't stand to see those Dodgers win the World Series. Those Dodgers have *never* won a World Series."

Applegate paused and rubbed his leg vigorously. "It seems late in the year for mosquitoes," he said.

"So you've gone out and bought yourself another hot shot."

"Right. Remember when we made our bargain last July? Well, at that time I was undecided for quite a while between you and another guy about your age. He's a television repairman, and as it turns out I should have picked him in the first place . . . not that it hasn't been a pleasure to know you, Joe. No hard feelings, you understand."

"But listen, the least you can do is give him another name."

"Can't, Joe. I realize it's kind of desecrating something to use Joe Hardy's name, but it can't be helped. It's a question of eligibility. You know . . . a guy has to have been with the team through a certain part of the season, whatever it is, for him to be eligible for the Series. So he has to be Joe Hardy or nobody. The guy's gonna look like you, talk like you, act like you . . . everything. What I'm asking you is this: to keep your peace about it and, incidentally, to let me have the combination to your locker. We couldn't get in."

Joe laughed, then fell silent, looking up at the stars, chewing on a blade of grass. Finally he said, "Maybe we could work a deal at that, App. How about releasing Lola?"

Applegate was silent in turn. "I can't do that, Joe. She has to be punished."

"Well then, I guess you know what my answer is. I guess I'll be calling quite a few newspapers tomorrow."

"You're not willing to do it for old time's sake?"

"You're taxing my old time's sake beyond endurance, old man," Joe said tauntingly.

He rose, stretched. "Well, App, I guess I'll be seeing you . . ."

"Wait a minute now—just wait a minute. You're always going some place. Now listen, Joe, first of all Lola doesn't even want to be released. Honestly. I'm not kidding you on that score. She doesn't want to be ugly, I'll admit, but she doesn't want to be released."

"All right, then—give her her looks back. Make her—" Joe paused and his voice broke slightly. "Make her the most beautiful girl in the world again. In fact," he went on, struck by an idea now, "this new Joe Hardy you're going to create—"

"No, Joe, it wouldn't be the same. She'd know the difference between you and him, even though you looked alike."

"Well, all right, tell her the truth, but tell her I tried my best for her, will you?" he said, his voice breaking again. "Tell her I did my best for her and that I'll never forget her."

Applegate did not reply for a few moments. Then he said, "Look out, Joe, you're getting emotional." Picking up his portable radio, he rose. "In fact I think I'm going to leave baseball alone after this season. It seems like everybody involved with baseball is too emotional. It gets me upset. Okay, Joe. You drive a hard bargain, but it's a deal."

"You promise Lola gets her looks back?"

"Sure I promise. You know I live up to a contract."

"Yes, I'll give you that much anyway."

"Well, Joe, then this is it. . . . Incidentally, I still think that plate umpire made a lousy call. You were out by a foot."

"No," Joe said. "I slid away from the catcher. I hooked the plate."

"I still say you were out, but it's all over now. So . . . Joe . . . I guess I'll never see you again. Well . . ." Applegate's own voice caught, and as if to cover up, he gave

Joe a resounding whack on the back. "So long, old pal. Will you shake?"

Joe grasped the familiar limp fish and said, "Your hand-shake's no better than it ever was."

"Well," Applegate said, "we all have our limitations." Then suddenly he was gone.

Joe looked right and left, but there was no trace, and then he muttered, "So long, App."

The pain in his leg was less now as he headed resolutely for home, rehearsing once again what he would tell Bess, what he would tell them at the office. He smiled, remembering that Bess was now a baseball fan. He walked faster. Bess, after all, was his wife. He smiled again. Bess and the bridge girls had tickets for the World Series. He knew that he would not go to the World Series. He might listen to a game or two, but . . .

It was peculiar. Already he was aware of it. He no longer felt a passion for baseball. It was a game he would always like, but he knew he could never again qualify as an avid fan. Perhaps because he had given the game so much. Perhaps because now he realized there were things more important . . . a woman's sacrifice, Lola's . . . and the way Bess's eyes had looked that day when she said perhaps she owed it to her husband to become a ball fan because it was a sore point between them. People got divorced for less cause, she had said.

He walked on, following the familiar route, heading up toward the bus stop, turning to the right up the long hill.

The house was dark. There was no bridge game tonight.

He approached slowly, with an eerie feeling. Except for the change in the weather, except that there was no sound of Old Man Everett watering his azaleas, this might be that same night in July.